2008

D0380945

Allison felt t............................e world receded in nothingness, her head exploded with spasms of pain. The next thing she felt was the chill of the water and slimy tentacles clawing at her face, choking her neck. Lakes had always been Allison's friends, now this one was the enemy—suffocating her, strangling her, doing its best to destroy her. But she couldn't let that happen. She flailed at the water, tried to disentangle her arms and legs from the clinging weeds.

Air. She needed air. She needed air now. Her head popped through the surface of the water only to be met by another blow, this time from the planks above her head. It was too dark to see anything, but Allison realized she must be trapped under the pier.

She stifled a scream for help which tried to erupt from her throat. She knew it would bring no help, and would only alert her assailant that she was still alive.

★

Previously published Worldwide Mystery titles by
HELEN GOODMAN

MURDER IN EDEN
TOXIC WASTE

THE BLUE GOOSE IS DEAD

HELEN GOODMAN

W⬤RLDWIDE®

TORONTO • NEW YORK • LONDON
AMSTERDAM • PARIS • SYDNEY • HAMBURG
STOCKHOLM • ATHENS • TOKYO • MILAN
MADRID • WARSAW • BUDAPEST • AUCKLAND

If you purchased this book without a cover you should be aware
that this book is stolen property. It was reported as "unsold and
destroyed" to the publisher, and neither the author nor the
publisher has received any payment for this "stripped book."

Dedicated to my brothers, Jim and Gene Nelson,
who have always inspired me.

THE BLUE GOOSE IS DEAD

A Worldwide Mystery/October 2008

First published by Alabaster Books.

ISBN-13: 978-0-373-26652-4
ISBN-10:   0-373-26652-9

Copyright © 2007 by Helen Goodman.
All rights reserved. No part of this book may be reproduced
or transmitted in any form or by any means, electronic or
mechanical, including photocopying, recording or by any
information storage and retrieval system, without permission
in writing from the publisher. For information, contact:
Alabaster Books, P.O. Box 401, Kernersville, North Carolina 27285 U.S.A.

This is a work of fiction. Names, characters, places and incidents are
either the product of the author's imagination or are used fictitiously,
and any resemblance to actual persons, living or dead, business
establishments, events or locales is entirely coincidental.

® and TM are trademarks of Harlequin Enterprises Limited.
Trademarks indicated with ® are registered in the United States
Patent and Trademark Office, the Canadian Trade Marks Office
and in other countries.

Printed in U.S.A.

Acknowledgments

Many thanks to the members of my critique groups: Dixie, Larry, Dave, Lynette, John, Emogene, Joanne, Nancy, Betty, Dorothy, and Diane. Your comments are invaluable. Special thanks to Patty for proofreading these pages.

ONE

THE SIGN DANGLED drunkenly by one rusty chain. Allison peered around from the passenger seat to see its message. *Welcome to the Blue Goose Lodge* was still readable even though parts of some letters were missing. The smaller inscription below was blurred and fuzzy, but she could make out the words: *swimming, boating, fishing, hunting.* The once proud blue goose shown flying above the water was now a mixture of faded peeling paint and the dirt brown of rotting boards. Allison decided the sign looked about as bad as she felt. Road construction delays stretched their hundred-mile trip out to over three hours. She was exhausted, cramped, and wondering what in the world she was doing spending her vacation at a resort that had been closed for years.

Catherine slowed the car and rolled down the windows. "At this point in the road," she said, "I'm always torn between my love for Lake Lucia and the anxiety of seeing Aunt Bess." She gave a slight shudder. "Maybe I shouldn't have asked you to come, Allison. It was selfish of me. Somehow I thought you might act as a buffer against the painful past. How foolish. There's no hiding from the past—or from the future."

Mentally, Allison agreed with her. She shouldn't have invited me and I shouldn't have accepted. But we're here and we might as well make the best of it. Allison pasted on her best optimist's smile. "Never mind, Cat. You said you were looking forward to seeing your cousins again. We're going to have a good time. There's nothing to worry about." Allison knew she was trying to reassure herself as well as Catherine.

Frankly, it didn't look like any vacation spot she'd ever seen before. Allison studied the rusty wire fence entangled with honeysuckle vines, Creeping Jenny, and scrubby brushwood. The narrow gutted driveway and a battered garbage can were the only signs of civilization. And judging from the stench radiating from the can, it awaited a much needed catharsis.

Allison reminded herself just why she was at this once-well-known lodge which now housed only one sick embittered old woman. It started with a simple girls-night-out dinner at The Golden Corral celebrating the last day of school. "I don't feel like cooking after spending the day cleaning bulletin boards and clearing out desks," Catherine said. "Want to try the all-you-can-eat buffet?"

"Why not? Neither of us has anyone at home to object."

Catherine apparently lived alone by choice. Allison did so because her husband had absconded years earlier and her two kids were in college. Most of the time she was fine with it. She could come and go as she liked, read until all hours, write her eccentric poetry without criticism, and go on crazy vacations. But once in a while loneliness would wash over her like a riptide, tearing at her soul. She fought the feeling with Snickers and jogging. They both soothed her spirit and placated her body.

That night, though, she was feeling good, just looking forward to a nice quiet summer at home, tending her flower beds and working on her tai chi. Connie and Dave had summer jobs and couldn't come home, but the three of them had made plans to spend a week together at Atlantic Beach in August.

Throughout the meal, Catherine kept telling Allison how much she dreaded going to the Blue Goose to see her aunt. Allison slathered more butter on her roll and gave her friend a quizzical look. "Why go at all if she makes you that uncomfortable?"

"I don't have much choice," Catherine said. "My cousins and I have been summoned to Lake Lucia for a week in June. Queen Bess has spoken and we must scurry to do her bidding." Catherine lifted her glass and took a sip of tea. The ice cubes started clanging against the sides of the glass like castanets, and she quickly set it back down. She dabbed her napkin at a wet spot on the table.

Since it didn't look like Catherine was going to say anything else, Allison took the lead. "So—is Queen a part of your aunt's name or an honorary title?"

Catherine grinned. "A title, I guess, though not

exactly honorary. Her lowly subjects bestowed it on her because she gave the orders and we were expected to obey them."

"And I assume you're referring to yourself and your cousins as the other lowly subjects."

"Yes. The cousins are Charles and Teddy. But they're not Aunt Bess's sons. She didn't have any kids." Catherine clasped her hands in front of her and wrinkled her nose. "It's pretty complicated. Besides, you're not interested in my problems."

"You know me better than that. I'm interested in everyone's problems. My curiosity is surpassed only by my nosiness." Allison shoved aside her empty plate and reached for dessert. She slipped her fork reverently into the Mississippi Mud Cake, lifted a morsel of the luscious chocolate-marshmallow mixture to her lips, half closed her eyes, and sighed in delight. "An offering fit for the gods," she said between swallows.

She looked up to see Catherine staring at her. "What?"

"Nothing. Just wondering how you can eat like a sumo wrestler and stay as thin as a broom."

"Simple. Exercise. Remember I'm a gym teacher."

"How could I forget? It's rumored that you're North Carolina's oldest girls' gym teacher. At least, that's what your students say behind your back."

"Adolescents think anyone over forty is ancient. But that's all right. It gets their attention and their respect. It just takes a while for the girls to get used to seeing a woman older than their mothers cavorting with a basketball." Allison wiped a bit of marshmallow from her lips. "But forget me. Since you're not having dessert, you talk and I'll eat. Just start at the beginning, Cat. Tell me all about your aunt, cousins, any other skeletons in your family closet. I'm all ears."

Catherine nodded. "All right, I will if you'll stop calling me by that ridiculous nickname."

"Well, it fits you. Your eyes are like a cat's. Soft, green eyes hiding secrets from the world."

Catherine laughed. "If you're expecting deep, dark secrets, you're going to be dreadfully disappointed."

Allison watched as Catherine leaned her head against the back of the booth. Her straw-colored hair blended with the beige cushion, and her hand trembled as she played with her fork. Allison knew Catherine was in her thirties, yet the face of the woman across from her seemed creased with care beyond her years.

Catherine took a deep breath. "Aunt Bess took me in after my parents were killed in an accident. I was ten at the time, an only child. She was my father's sister. She gave me a home, sent me to a private boarding school, and then to college. Even bought my first car. I owe her. I owe her big time."

"But you dislike her."

"It's not that exactly. It's just that I could never please her and I stopped trying years ago. I always felt like an intruder in her life."

A smile came into Catherine's voice with her next words. "My only happy memories at the Blue Goose are the summers. That's when my cousins came to visit."

"So now we come to the cousin part. Tell me about them."

"Their father was Bess's other brother. Charles is a year older than I am, and Teddy two years younger. We had some great times together. When their dad died, Aunt Bess footed the bills for them to go to college also."

"So they owe her too?"

"Yes."

"And they dislike her too?"

"I guess so. We never really discussed her in those terms. But we made fun of her and called her Queen Bess—except when Derita was around."

"And where does Derita fit in?" Allison asked.

"She was Uncle Henry's niece, about our age. Uncle Henry was Aunt Bess's husband. He was killed in a boating accident shortly after I came to live at the lodge. Derita's parents are still living and quite well off. She's not really a cousin to the rest of us, but we gave her that honor. She spent a lot of her vacations at the lodge. She and I had our disagreements about the importance of clothes and boyfriends and dancing lessons, but most of the time we got along well. The strange thing is— Derita is the only one who doesn't owe Aunt Bess anything and she's the only one that seems to like her."

"I'm glad somebody likes her. Besides, maybe she's mellowed since you've last seen her."

"Maybe. And maybe we'll have snow for the Fourth of July." Catherine took both hands and lifted her glass of tea to take a sip, but still the glass trembled.

Allison was puzzled. What was making Catherine so nervous? There's more here than she's telling me. I think there really are secrets hiding in those eyes.

"Actually," Catherine said. "Aunt Bess is better natured when strangers are around. Do come with me. I need you."

And never let it be said that Allison Aldridge deserted a friend in need. So here they were heading toward the Blue Goose Lodge and the infamous aunt. The driveway snaked through tangled underbrush. Allison caught glimpses of playful squirrels and curious chipmunks, but no buildings came into view. "And just where are you hiding this lovely lodge?" she asked.

"Around the bend, down the hill, and behind a barricade of loblolly pines." Catherine named the landmarks as the car slowly wound its way down. The lodge loomed into sight. "I always thought it looked like a fortress tethered loosely to the hillside," she said, "just waiting for the right moment to loosen its grip and slide silently into the still water below."

Allison studied the bulky gray edifice that looked like it may have escaped from the cover of a Gothic Romance book. Dozens of windows peered out at her, most of them draped in dark curtains. She wondered if they were meant to keep the sunlight out, or to keep secrets in. Turrets topped each corner of the lodge maintaining watch over the grounds, and a grand cupola arose on the roof. A giant chimney on the far side brooded over the structure. "You didn't tell me it was a spooky mansion," she mumbled.

"Must have slipped my mind. But don't worry. The vampires only come out during the full moon and we keep Dracula carefully chained in the cellar."

Allison gave a nervous laugh. "If that was meant to comfort me, it fell a little short. But thanks for trying."

"No problem."

"But why is it so overgrown? Bushes, vines, weeds gone wild everywhere? Your aunt must not believe in landscaping."

"After Uncle Henry died and the paying guests stopped coming, I guess she decided to let it go back au naturel. She just keeps the patch of lawn mowed from the front of the house down to the lake." As Catherine said this, the driveway took a sudden turn to the right and Lake Lucia came into view. Catherine stopped the car and took a deep breath. "It always catches me by surprise. The lake looks so beautiful, so serene."

They gazed at the tranquil scene in silence. The late morning sun bathed the water in gaudy sequins. Lazy waves, made by a distant boat, slapped the shoreline with a muffled thud. A lone heron guarded the dock. Standing on one spindly leg, he stretched, ruffled his feathers, dove into the water. Then he surfaced and glided slowly over the lake, searching for an early lunch.

"Oh, Cat, it's lovely. Like a piece of paradise."

"Like the old song says, *Nothing could be finer than to be in Caroliner in the morning.* Or something like that." Catherine's smile faded. "Unfortunately, my singing mood doesn't extend to the rest of the place."

Allison's eyes drifted across the water to the other side of the lake. The nearly solid green was pierced only occasionally by tiny white cottages and miniature log cabins. "Doesn't look like many people live around here."

"No, we're pretty isolated. That's the way Uncle Henry wanted it when the lodge was open. I think people came here to get away from the crowds. There's scattered campgrounds around the lake now, but they're pretty much back in the woods. And there's no cell phone reception either so we're pretty much in the dark ages."

Catherine started the car and they rounded another curve which brought the front yard into their sight. It was evident it hadn't seen a lawnmower in weeks. The grass and weeds looked knee-high. "Maybe your Aunt Bess has decided to let the yard go back to the wild, also," Allison said.

Catherine stared at the matted grass. "I can't believe this. She always had a boy from town cut the grass every week. I'll see about it as soon as we get unpacked. We can't live in a jungle like that."

The driveway swung around behind the house into a large parking area once filled with many guests' vehicles. Most of the area now had been reclaimed by the nearby woods leaving space for only a half-dozen cars. Catherine drove up next to a new canary-yellow convertible. "Derita beat us here," she announced. "No one else I know would drive a car like that."

As they were heaving their luggage out of the trunk, the owner of the convertible emerged from the back door of the house. She stood waiting on the steps until Catherine glanced up and saw her. Then she gave a poster-girl smile and stretched out her arms. Catherine dropped one bag, gave Derita a half-wave and said, "How about making yourself useful for a change?"

Derita descended the steps and reached for a bag. "Good to see you too, Cousin."

Allison stopped midway to the house, a suitcase in each hand and a puzzled stare for the two women. What was going on here?

Then Catherine and Derita both dropped their bags, gave a lunge, and collapsed giggling into each other's arms. Their words collided as they squealed and hugged each other.

"I'm so glad you're here."

"You look great."

When they had regained their composure, Catherine made the introductions. "Allison, this is Derita Lattimer or whatever name she's going by now. I can't keep up with her husbands." Catherine rolled her eyes at Derita. "How many have you gone through now?"

"Three. But who's counting? Besides, since you

refuse to play the marriage game I figure I have to take up the slack."

"Very commendable of you. Anyway, this is Allison Aldridge, a fellow teacher. I brought her along to give you a lesson in humility. She'll out-swim, out-tennis and out-horseshoe you."

Derita reached for Allison's hand. "It'll be a pleasure to have some real competition. Beating Catherine isn't even fun anymore."

Catherine gave Derita another hug. "You really do look great, as usual." Catherine turned to Allison. "Derita did some fashion modeling in college and ever since then she's kept wearing the same styles. Her husbands may change, but never her hairdo or her clothes."

Allison understood what Catherine meant. Derita was definitely retro. She was wearing khaki shorts, topped by a clinging blouse and a linen jacket the color of burnt sugar. Her waist, so small it looked like it had been squeezed by a vise, was encircled with gold chains. Her frosted hair was tangled just enough to suggest the windblown look, and an array of rings adorned most of her fingers. The flamingo pink of her fingernails was duplicated on her toenails that peeked coyly through the ends of huarache sandals. She was the perfect picture of past elegance.

"You look good too, Catherine," she said. "You always look so—comfortable."

"Thanks," Catherine said with a grin, "but I think the correct word is drab."

Again Allison concurred. Catherine was wearing

baggy jeans, tee shirt, scruffy Keds, scant makeup and had her hair pulled back in a pony tail. Of course, Allison wasn't being critical since she was dressed in a similar costume. The main difference was that Allison's hair was cropped short befitting her athletic life.

Derita opened the door and, as she did, a cat, the color of an October pumpkin, streaked into the house. "Wait a minute, Lancelot," Derita yelped as she scrambled after the disappearing feline. "You don't belong in there." While Derita was chasing the cat, Catherine and Allison managed to get their bags inside the door. After a few anguished cries, the captured trespasser was evicted. "And stay out." Derita's voice followed the cat outside as she brushed off some offending cat hair and inspected her hands for scratches.

"But that's not Lancelot," Catherine objected.

"It is now. Aunt Bess said the first Lancelot died and Jake got her this cat to take his place. But she kept the same name. The trouble is she can't have a cat in the house now with her worsening asthma and this Lancelot doesn't take to being an outside cat. Every time the door opens he tries to sneak in."

Forgetting her status as a guest, Allison defended the cat. "Well, you didn't have to toss him out like he was a piece of garbage. He probably just likes to be around people." Slipping out the door, Allison got down on her knees and started coaxing the cat. Lancelot had taken refuge behind a clump of yellow daisies where his orange fur blended in nicely.

"Come here, Kitty. Come to Allison. I won't hurt you." In a few moments the wary cat reached out his nose to meet her fingers halfway. "That's a good boy, Lancelot. You and I are going to be friends."

Catherine laughed. "Allison, you could make friends with an attack dog." Turning to Derita, Catherine said, "Speaking of friends, have you seen dear Jake since you've been here?"

"Oh, yes. He was visiting Aunt Bess when I arrived two days ago. He was hanging onto her every word, worrying she might be too cool with the windows open, telling her she mustn't get overly tired. And when he left he instructed me to take good care of my dear auntie. I assured him I would."

Allison reentered the house and the conversation. She realized it was going to take some doing to keep up with everything going on here at the Blue Goose, and she was determined to do it. "Now who is dear Jake?" she asked. "Like they say in baseball, you have to know the players to keep up with the game."

"And I wouldn't want you to miss out on any of the game," Derita said. "Jake is Aunt Bess's oldest and dearest friend."

Catherine interrupted, "You forgot to mention that he's probably her only friend."

"Now Catherine," Derita said, "that's not fair. Aunt Bess is very well thought of around the lake as well as in town."

Catherine gave Derita a wry smile. "I stand corrected." She turned to Allison and explained, "Jake's been around since the dawn of creation and will probably outlast all of us. He lives cater-corner around the lake, ten minutes by rowboat or a good hour's walk through the woods. He's kind and gentle." Catherine paused and smirked at her cousin, "In other words, he has nothing in common with our aunt. The boys and I used to say that Aunt Bess put a spell on Jake so he couldn't see her evil nature."

"Actually," Derita whispered, "Catherine thinks she put an evil spell on all of us. We're helpless to fight against her."

Allison picked up a suitcase and looked up the stairs. "I'm not sure if I should unpack, or steal a car and head back home."

"Don't let us bother you, Allison," Derita said. "We may be a little strange, but I assure you we're completely harmless."

A FEW MILES FROM lovely Lake Lucia lies the county seat of Webster. It's a small town with quiet streets, a county courthouse dating from the early 1800s, numerous churches, a spattering of gas stations, diners, and antique shops. The sheriff's office and county jail occupies a recent addition to the back of the courthouse. Behind the front desk, a long hallway leads to various offices. The last door on the right is the domain of Detective Fred Sawyer.

Fred glanced at his desk calendar. The last days of May had scuttled away, inching open the door for summer. Summer—another sizzling, clammy, deodorant-defying North Carolina summer. And it didn't matter how stupid hot it got, county detectives were expected to answer their calls wearing a suit and tie. Admittedly, if he was required to stay away from air-conditioning for any length of time, he would causally loosen his tie and even slip off his jacket, but that was still a long way from being comfortable. And the older he got, the more Fred liked comfort. Of course, he didn't consider fifty-three old, but it was old enough to know what really counted in life. Comfort counted.

He slipped a letter out from under the dappled blotter. Nowadays, he thought, there weren't many ink stains for blotters to soak up, but they still served a purpose. They were perfect for cushioning frosty cans of Mountain Dew, sopping up sloshed coffee, and welcoming the doodles of stumped investigators.

The letter lay heavily on his hand, not because of its actual weight, but because of its weighty contents. It stated, in bureaucratic language, that he had contributed thirty years of his life in the county's service and was now eligible for retirement. It was tempting— a summer in Bermuda shorts, his RV, the Great Smokies, maybe even Yellowstone. Even as he visualized the joys of camping next to a gurgling stream, an inner voice interrupted with, *Alone? You want to do this alone?*

That's what stopped him. There was no Mrs. Sawyer waiting in the wings to join him in a Huck Finn holiday, no girlfriend he could invite.

He shoved the letter back. Maybe one more summer, one more year. One more good murder.

TWO

Derita picked up one of the bags. "Let me help you get settled, Allison. You can have my old room so you'll be next to Catherine."

"You don't have to give up your room," Catherine said.

"We can put Allison in the haunted bell tower."

"That won't work. I already have a boyfriend stashed up there, but I told him he couldn't come out until midnight." Allison threw up her hands. "Okay, you two. Cut the horseplay and just give me a bed so I can crash. I've got to figure out how I can survive in this madhouse."

Derita's face sobered and she turned to Catherine. "My old room is empty anyway, so Allison may as well have it. Aunt Bess insisted I stay in the room next to her so there would be someone close by. It's her night nurse's room, but Aunt Bess gave her the week off while we're here."

"I didn't know Aunt Bess had a nurse. Is she really that sick?"

"I'm afraid so. Of course, she denies it. She needs to be in a nursing home but refuses to consider it."

Catherine grabbed another suitcase and started up the stairs. "We could use the elevator," she told

Allison, "but the stairs are quicker. Let's get these to our rooms, and then you can meet Queen Bess."

"Fine," Allison agreed. "Just point me in the right direction."

At the top of the stairs, she tagged along behind the cousins. "Your room is toward the back of the lodge," Derita informed her. "It looks out on what we used to call 'the forest of the night creatures.'"

"Oh, thanks." Allison shuddered at the thought. "That should give me something sweet to dream about!"

"Well, it beats the other side of the hall where the boys will be," Catherine said. "They're over the tennis court, but in the distance you can hear what goes on in the Blackwood Believers' cemetery."

"I didn't see a cemetery when we drove in."

"You can't see it from our road and the only way to it is nearly grown over," Derita said. "The church hasn't been open for years and is beginning to crumble. But those Blackwood repentant ghosts are still busy praying and wailing. There's no mistaking them when the wind is in the right direction."

"I can tell I'm in for a restful vacation." Allison made her way down the hall. "And what view do you have now, Derita?"

"The lake, of course. The peaceful, serene lake."

When the suitcases were deposited, Derita turned back toward the stairs. "You'd better scoot on down, Catherine, and pay your respects. Aunt Bess knows you're here and will be wondering what's taking you so long."

"I think I'll unpack first and show Allison around."

"All right, but Auntie isn't going to be happy with you."

"She never is."

Back downstairs, Catherine steered Allison over to what had been the cousins' recreation room. "This was originally a card room for the guests, but Aunt Bess let us convert it for our use. We decorated it ourselves."

Allison surveyed the room with approval. It reminded her of her own basement that her kids had renovated. Both rooms were suspended in a "teen time-warp." There was a TV, a ping-pong table, and shelves of "young adult" books guarded by a menagerie of stuffed animals. There were classic movie posters of *Casablanca* and *Gone With the Wind* mingled with *The Karate Kid* and *Grease*. One wall was covered with 'paint-by-number' pictures: clowns, old barns peeking through snow, birds in flight. Another wall held a dart board surrounded by tiny holes where darts had not only missed the target, but the entire board. The hardwood floor was speckled with mysterious stains which had probably started out as mustard, strawberry jelly and grape Kool-Aid.

"Nice." Allison said. "I'm sure you had some good times here."

Catherine nodded. "Here we felt free to laugh, to dance, to be young. But we had to keep the door closed so we wouldn't disturb Aunt Bess who seldom laughed, never danced and who, we were sure, could never have been young."

"Aren't you being a little hard on her? After all, she gave you a lot."

"Yeah. Sure. Well, you'll meet her in a little bit, and she can dazzle you with her charming personality. But, first I want to show you the billiard room."

Catherine led the way down the hall to the front of the house. She opened a pair of heavily curtained French doors and they entered an adult recreation room. A billiard table dominated one end of the room while a massive fireplace prevailed at the other end. The timbered walls on either side of the hearth displayed antlered heads of powerful bucks, a huge mounted largemouth bass, and a stuffed red fox with his bushy tail flying out behind him. "Uncle Henry's collection," Catherine explained. "I think he liked to impress his sporting guests."

Beneath the fox was a liquor cabinet, which still looked well stocked. "And, of course, after the hunt there was much celebrating. I doubt the cabinet has even been opened since Uncle Henry's death. Aunt Bess left everything in here just the way it was."

"Perhaps a memorial to him?"

"Perhaps. Or maybe she just didn't want to be bothered with it."

Catherine pivoted around and pointed to a circular staircase nearly hidden behind the billiard table. "That was our escape route."

"Escape route? Escape from what?"

"From Aunt Bess's eyes and ears. Until her health

became so bad, she would have her bridge club over regularly. On those nights, we were banned to our rooms upstairs and told not to disturb the adults. On those same nights, the idea of a late night swim became irresistible. We couldn't use the back stairway as it could be seen from the dining room where the card players sat. So we would sneak down these stairs, slip into the hallway, dash out the front door and down to the lake. We could have our swim and be back in the house before the card game ended. It was great fun!"

Allison nodded her head in agreement. "Sounds like."

"Of course, Derita was hesitant about disobeying orders, but Teddy said, 'It's not wrong if we don't get caught.'" Catherine frowned. "Somehow, at the time, that rationale made sense."

They retraced their steps down the hallway. "Aunt Bess spends her days in the library," Catherine said, "but let's go through the kitchen first. I want you to meet Lillian. She's been the cook and housekeeper at the Blue Goose for more than thirty years. When I first arrived here, Lillian headed up a staff of six, kept everybody fed and everything clean without a wasted step or a wasted smile. When the paying customers and other staff left, Lillian stayed on with no loss of efficiency. Her smiles only increased during the summers when Teddy showed up. Something about Teddy made Lillian want to pet him, protect him and, most of all, feed him. I guess it was because he was small for his age and as skinny as a fishing pole. If we ever wanted a late night snack, a picnic lunch, or a special dessert, we always sent Teddy to make the request. Lillian never refused him anything.

"In recent years Lillian has begun to slow down and Aunt Bess hired Serena, a young girl from town, to ease the load. Serena comes to fix breakfast each morning and does Aunt Bess's bidding on weekends. Lillian works weekdays from about ten until after dinner."

The kitchen door stood open, but Catherine tapped to get Lillian's attention. The cook greeted Catherine with restrained enthusiasm. "Well, it's about time you got here."

Catherine gave her a hug and introduced Allison. "Lillian is one of the best cooks south of the Mason-Dixon line. Her sweet-potato pies consistently won blue ribbons at the county fair. You're in for an eating good time this week."

"Pay her no mind, Allison. I'm just a plain country cook. Nothing fancy comes out of this kitchen, but I do guarantee you won't go hungry."

"Sounds good to me." Allison decided Lillian probably enjoyed indulging in her own cooking and as a consequence she could politely be called "rotund." Her hair sported a black, shoe-polish look that Allison surmised was a home color treatment.

Catherine threaded her way through the kitchen and sniffed appreciatively. "Smells good. What is it?"

"Chicken stew."

"Of course, Teddy's favorite. Bet you made banana pudding too."

Lillian scowled and nodded. "Teddy enjoys good cooking—and it's a cinch he doesn't get any at home."

"Now why do you think that? I'm sure Imogene knows her way around a stove." I could tell Cath--erine enjoyed teasing Lillian. The older woman, though, had no smile on her face.

"Humph, that woman? Imogene's so busy with her theater group she doesn't even know what a kitchen looks like. Calls herself an actress! Let me tell you about her acting. I visited my sister in Char-lotte last fall when Imogene was in one of those community theater plays. So I called Teddy and he took me to the play. It was supposed to be a comedy, but I didn't see much funny about it. People jumping in and out of bed and getting caught in closets and losing their underwear. Why, Imogene came on stage once wearing nothing but a skimpy slip! Teddy was so proud of her, but I'd seen better acting when my granddaughter played Little Red Riding Hood."

Lillian stopped talking long enough to give the stew a quick stir. She stared at Catherine through the ensuing steam. Slamming the lid back on the bubbling pot, Lillian shook the spoon at Catherine. "Oh, Imogene's pretty all right, but that's not enough to build an acting career on."

Catherine swiped the spoon and licked the gravy dripping down its handle. Lillian grabbed the spoon back and tossed it in the sink. She was too intent on her story to even scold Catherine. "Teddy told me he was investing money in a play and that Imogene was going to be the star. I told him he was just throwing his money away." Lillian sighed. "I don't know why he loves that girl so much, when all she cares about is her acting and her fancy jewelry. But, I declare, I do think Teddy would do anything for her."

Allison was fascinated by Lillian's tirade against Imogene. The cook certainly made no bones about her dislike of Teddy's wife. Catherine must have decided she'd heard enough and changed the subject. "How's Aunt Bess today?"

Lillian grabbed the dishcloth and wiped a speck of chicken from the counter. "Not good. But then, you know, she's not one to complain. She has her array of pills and sprays and inhalers that keep her going. Get yourself in there now and see her. But don't start a fuss."

Catherine's face paled. "I'm not the one who starts the fusses," she said. Lillian turned her back, and Catherine headed for the library. Allison was close behind.

Bess Lattimer was sitting by the window that gave a view of the tennis court. She was leaning back in her recliner and had her eyes closed. Allison studied Catherine studying her aunt. Her face was hard to read. Was it worry, sadness, or contempt?

Allison found it easier to read the old woman. She concluded the past few years had not treated Bess kindly. Her apparently robust frame had shriveled, and her face resembled a corrugated box. Her gray hair was short and frizzy, with pink scalp peeking through on top. She wore a royal-blue housecoat with a blue and gold shawl drawn tightly around her shoulders. A multicolored afghan covered her legs. Allison admired the bright colors, but they only made the woman's skin look more pallid.

Even in rest Bess seemed to struggle for each shallow breath. She stirred and groaned. Catherine reached for her hand and shivered slightly. Bess opened her eyes and Catherine squeezed her aunt's hand, but at the same time her own hands were trembling. She smiled brightly, "Hi, Aunt Bess. So good of you to invite me."

Her aunt gave a wry grin and in an amazingly strong voice said, "So good of you to come." At the end of the sentence a noisy wheezing sound escaped, followed by an even louder wheeze when the old woman tried to inhale.

Catherine glanced at the inhaler on the windowsill. She reached toward it. "Need this?"

With a deep gasp Bess shook her head, brushed Catherine's hand away, then seized the blue inhaler herself like a drowning man grabbing for a life preserver. After several seconds the wheezing subsided and a touch of pink colored her sunken cheeks. Her next words came out in short spurts. "I've gotten along…without your help…for years. Don't need it now." Catherine kept her smile in place and made no comment. Bess gave her a disapproving stare and went on, "Why do you insist…on tying your hair…back like that? It just emphasizes…your big ears."

Catherine continued to smile, but her eyes turned

away from the invalid. "I'm on vacation. I really don't care how I look."

"You never did. I'm afraid to think…how you dress for your students."

"I don't dress for my students," Catherine snapped. The smile was gone. "I'm there to teach them, not to give a fashion show."

"Of course. But enough of that. You've seen Derita?"

"Yes. She said she arrived a couple of days ago."

"That's right. And she's been hovering over me…like a seeing eye dog. Insisted I give my nurse a week off…announced that she would sleep in the room…next to mine. I don't need a nurse in the first place. I only have her to satisfy Dr. Caldwell. He thinks I shouldn't be alone. Drat foolishness. I've always taken care of myself." The long speech took its toll and it was several moments before the gasping and wheezing abated.

Lillian peeked in from the kitchen. "I'll run up and get your noon meds, Bess."

"It's five to twelve," her employer grumbled. "You should have already…had them down here." Lillian dashed out of the room.

The lull gave Catherine the chance to introduce Allison, who had been standing in the shadows and now stepped forward.

"Aunt Bess, I'd like you to meet a friend of mine from school. This is Allison Aldridge. She's…"

Whatever else Catherine had planned to say was interrupted by another wheezing spell. Bess nodded to Allison, but turned her attention back to her niece and gasped. "Well, I'm glad you've finally been able…to make some friends."

Catherine turned away and swallowed hard. At that moment Allison understood exactly why Catherine had dreaded coming to the Blue Goose. It's seldom that Allison would take an instant dislike to a person, but Bess Lattimer pushed every mean button in her body. She shoved ahead of Catherine and grasped the old witch's hand. She was determined to be as sweet as Bess was ugly. It was what Solomon called heaping coals of fire on your enemy's head. "I'm so pleased to meet you, Mrs. Lattimer. Catherine told me a lot about you, but she didn't mention your delightful sense of humor, or your fierce independence. I really admire a person who refuses to be mollycoddled." Allison thought she heard Catherine choking behind her, but she continued her assault of kindness. "And you certainly don't look like you need to have a nurse hanging around. I can't imagine what that doctor is thinking about. Like you said, just drat foolishness."

By this time Bess was staring at Allison as if she were a schizophrenic off her medicine. "But…but," she gasped.

Allison didn't give Bess a chance to continue, as she launched another salvo. "And I'm so glad someone around here has a sense of fashion. That housecoat is simply gorgeous and the brilliant blue complements the reds and oranges in the afghan. Catherine and I certainly could take some lessons from you."

Allison was about to run out of palaver and was grateful when Lillian returned to the room. She had her hands full of pill bottles that she aligned on the windowsill within Bess's reach. Bess grabbed the closest one, shook two tablets into her shaking hands and seized her glass of water.

"Well, it's been nice…talking to you," Bess said. "Now I'm sure you…want to wash up before lunch."

"Yes, Allison," Catherine said. "We really must get washed up." She snatched her friend's arm and pulled her toward the door. Allison could tell Catherine was doing her best to hold back her laughter. Lillian glared at both of them. The sound of a car broke the spell.

"That must be Teddy and Imogene," Lillian said. "I'll serve lunch as soon as they get settled. If I don't, that boy will be in my kitchen giving me a fit. He's always hungry. Poor thing."

After greetings and hugs between the cousins, Aunt Bess took her place at the head of the table. Derita sat on her right side, followed by Catherine and Allison. Teddy and Imogene sat on the other side. Catherine smiled across at her cousin. Allison remembered Catherine telling her that Teddy had always been the mischievous one of the bunch: the one who dared to swim the furthest, to dive the deepest, to climb the highest. Allison was drawn to the impish grin and the devilish eyes, but at the same time she sensed a shrewdness there that was anything but childlike.

"Looks like life is treating you well, Teddy," Catherine said. "You're hale and hearty."

Teddy grinned. "Maybe a little too hearty. I keep pretty busy, but I manage to squeeze in three square meals a day."

"Or four," Imogene said, patting her husband's belt. She puckered her lips in what Allison supposed was meant to be a cute pout. "There's some of us, though, who have to watch our figures. The stage is such a demanding taskmaster."

Allison wasn't sure if the line was intended to be funny or not. Probably not. Apparently Imogene took her acting with great seriousness. Allison studied Imogene's figure and wondered how such big boobs could fit in the same body with an anorexic waist. She suspected there might have been a little uplifting surgery in the past. She had to admit Imogene's appearance was striking: ink-black, shoulder-length hair carefully arranged in tangled curls with soft bangs which caressed full eyebrows. Dark mascara clung to thick lashes while her lips were embossed with palest pink. Imogene reminded Allison of a doll—a cold porcelain doll, one that was meant to be admired but never played with.

"I thought Charles would be here by now," Teddy said between bites. "When I talked to him last week, he said he planned to leave early this morning."

Bess made a motion with her right hand to Derita indicating for her to tell the news. Apparently it took too much effort for Bess to eat and talk at the same time.

"Oh, yes," Derita said. "He did leave early, but called and said he had decided to bring the kids. He was going by to pick them up and will be here later this afternoon."

"That's great!" Catherine said. "It's been two years since I've seen those youngsters." Turning to Allison, she explained, "Charles is divorced and the kids live with their mother, so I don't see them often. You're going to love them. Becky's twelve now and Wesley is almost ten. They're both wildcats."

"So I'll have someone to play with? I was wondering what I was going to do with just grownups around."

"Well, I hope Becky has grown up a little bit," Derita said. "Maybe by now she knows what a dress is."

"I doubt it," Imogene chimed in. "Charles brought them by last fall when he attended a conference called 'Save the Planet' or 'Help the Earth' or some such crazy name. Anyway, the kids were only interested in recycling, saving the rain forests and something about reducing the use of fossil fuels. Half the time I couldn't understand what they were talking about. Charles has filled their head with all this environmental nonsense. I tried to get Becky to let me fix her hair and put on a little makeup, but she would have none of it."

Teddy reached over and patted his wife's hand, "Don't fret, Honey. You did your best. There are some people you just can't civilize."

"That's right," Catherine said, aiming her voice to the head of the table. "Aunt Bess has been trying to civilize me for years."

Bess ignored the remark, and Derita gave Catherine a sly grin. "We gave up on you long ago. But maybe Charles and his kids aren't beyond rescuing."

"I don't know," Teddy said. "Charles may have already gone over the deep end. He's joined a group that's lobbying Washington to stop offshore drilling. He's just not thinking straight these days."

"I know all about Charles's thinking." Bess had finished her chicken stew and was now able to talk. "He wants me to give some property to the Nature Conservancy."

Forks stopped in midair, jaws dropped, eyes widened, and silence hovered over the table. Finally Teddy said, "But Aunt Bess, we thought that was settled long ago. You said you were leaving everything equally to the four of us, and that we could decide later about selling—or whatever."

"I've changed my mind. I've decided what to do with the lodge. And my land. We'll discuss it when Charles gets here. Until then I'm going to get some rest." The old woman rose, pulled her shawl tighter around her bent shoulders, and shuffled to the library and her recliner.

Allison glanced from one face to the other. She could tell the cousins were startled and concerned about their aunt's statement. She figured that each one of them had their own private agenda about what should happen to the Blue Goose and its adjoining acreage. A sudden chill seemed to intrude on the sunny June day, and Allison had an uneasy feeling about the upcoming meeting.

As the cousins left the dining room, Catherine hung behind. "You go ahead, Allison," she said. "I'll be along in a minute. I need to talk to Aunt Bess."

Allison waited in the hallway outside the library door. She didn't mean to eavesdrop, but couldn't help overhearing Catherine say, "I need a few more moments of your time, Aunt Bess."

"I'm not going to discuss the lodge now."

"It's not about the lodge." Catherine paused. "I…." Allison heard her take a deep breath. "I just want to be sure you've kept your promise. That is, you haven't told anyone about my mother?"

Bess snorted. "No. I haven't told a soul. I'm just as ashamed of her as you are."

"I'm not ashamed of her." Allison thought she detected a sob in Catherine's voice. "I just wish things could have been different."

Her aunt's voice hardened. "We take what life deals us. You, of all people, should know that by now. No need to whimper about it."

Catherine slipped out the door without replying. Allison noticed tears in her friend's eyes and her whole body was quivering.

"You were wrong," she said when she caught sight of Allison. "I don't dislike Aunt Bess." She swiped at her eyes, tossed her head back. "I purely gut *hate* her."

THREE

AFTER LUNCH the cousins scattered. Derita drove to town, Teddy and Imogene decided to take a walk in the woods, and Catherine determined to tackle the front yard. Allison was surprised that none of them seemed to want to discuss the next meeting of the clan.

Eliciting Allison's help, Catherine started toward the garage behind the parking lot. "I think the lawnmower's still in good shape. Apparently Aunt Bess hasn't been able to hire anyone to cut the yard this year."

"No problem. You and I can get it done in no time and then cool off in the lake."

"That's what I'd hoped you'd say. So let's get pushing."

"Pushing? What do you mean, Cat? No riding mower?"

Catherine shook her head. "If you tried riding on a yard with this much slope you'd end up in the lake sooner than you wanted."

Finding the lawnmower was easy; pulling it out from behind a ladder and a wheelbarrow loaded with old paint cans wasn't. "Aunt Bess gave up driving years ago," Catherine said, "so now the garage is used to store stuff which should be thrown away."

When they started mowing, it didn't take long for them to realize they'd taken on a tough task. One trip across the matted overgrown yard was all Catherine could manage before calling for relief. "This is going to take longer than I thought. It's like trying to mow through a haystack."

Allison grabbed the mower and started back on the next lap. They continued to switch back and forth, but before the yard was even half mowed, the two women were nearly exhausted. "Some vacation this has turned out to be," Allison muttered as she turned the growling machine around. "I swear this yard gets bigger every time I go across it." Catherine gave a sympathetic smile, but was too tired to comment.

Before Allison could get started back across, a husky voice swiveled them both around. "Hey, neighbors. Looks like you could use some help." Her first impression was that the ancient statue of Zeus had come alive, traveled all the way from Greece, and landed on the lakeshore. She quickly amended the picture. This god did have on a few more clothes and his beard was neatly trimmed.

Catherine caught her breath. "You got that right. We surely could use some help." She held out an only slightly trembling hand. "I'm Catherine Faircloth, a damsel in distress. And I assume you're a knight in shining armor."

"Absolutely. Name's Paul Daggert. I'm next door."

"Next door? Last I knew there wasn't a house within shouting distance, and certainly not close enough to hear a lawn mower."

"There is now. Not exactly a house, but a temporary abode." He stretched his hand out toward the lake to the left of the Lattimer boathouse. "Go right through those sycamores, past some wild grape vines and you'll come to my Winabago travel trailer, along with my borrowed pontoon boat. I'm renting that point of land for a week. It's right on the edge of this property."

As Paul talked, Allison reveled in the deep masculine voice while Catherine appeared to be studying the rest of him. Allison wondered if she noticed the way the sun gleamed on his copper-red beard, how the sweat glistened down his brawny arms and how the too-tight Bermuda shorts hugged his upper legs. At school Catherine had never shown much interest in the opposite sex and had rebuffed any of Allison's attempts to pair her with the single band director or the newly divorced football coach. But surely, Allison thought, she couldn't ignore this perfect male specimen.

He looked from one to the other. "Are you two Mrs. Lattimer's nieces?"

"Yes," Catherine nodded quickly. "That is, I am. You know my aunt?"

"No. But I know of her. And I was told her nieces and nephews would be visiting this week. The real estate agent was also telling me that her land might be up for sale soon. Any truth to it?"

Catherine didn't answer the question, but proceeded with proper introductions. "I'm her niece, and this is my friend, Allison Aldridge."

Allison pushed the wailing lawnmower away and shook Paul's hand. "Did I hear an offer of help?" She liked his schoolboy smile and noticed that his soft eyes matched the waters of Lake Lucia. And when she noticed his bare ring finger, her matchmaking juices started to flow. She glanced from Paul to Catherine and back again. *Ah, here's a situation that may lead to something.* "Well," Allison said, "back to work. I'll make another round while you two get acquainted."

"Not so fast," Paul said. "I came over here to help and that's what I'm going to do. You two lovely ladies wait here and watch a master at work." The bearded giant took off across the yard behind the mighty mower. They gazed in admiration as man and machine turned an unkept jungle into a respectable lawn.

He'd just finished when the porch screen-door slammed, and two wild Indians yahooed down the hill. They crashed into Catherine and all three rolled on the ground, shrieking and giggling. "Okay, enough already," Catherine panted. "Let me up or I'll drown you both when we get in the lake."

When she untangled herself, Catherine introduced her cousin's children to Paul and Allison. "This beautiful princess with the wild haircut is Becky and underneath all that tan is Wesley."

"Come on," Wesley cried out, "let's get our swim suits on. Last one in the water is a rotten egg."

Catherine turned back as she was being dragged away. "You're coming too, aren't you, Paul? Allison and I may need your help."

Paul nodded. "I wouldn't miss it. I'll meet you at the pier."

They'd been swimming much too short a time when Charles came down to the water's edge. "Sorry to cut this short, Catherine, but Aunt Bess is ready for our meeting now." Reluctantly Catherine swam toward shore.

"We don't have to get out, do we, Daddy?" Becky called.

Allison waved her hand. "We haven't met yet, Charles, but I'm Allison and you can trust the children with me. Just ask Cat—Catherine."

"And I'm Paul," a red-bearded mouth spoke up. "Cat will vouch for me too." Catherine stopped drying long enough to shake her head at both of them.

"Hey, kids," Paul shouted, "how about a ride on my pontoon? All right with you, Charles?" Charles nodded his assent and Catherine gave a last yearning look at the lake. Paul called out to her, "And I'll give you a private ride later, Cat." Catherine's face turned red as she trudged up the hill.

LATER IN THE AFTERNOON Catherine reported every detail of the family meeting to Allison. She wanted to vent her frustration and Allison let her talk. Allison had no trouble picturing the scene as Catherine described each person, each action, each nuance.

Charles entered the library, as he did every room, positive his presence would be as welcome as sunlight on a gloomy day. He'd always been the charmer of the family. This afternoon he gave his aunt and cousins the appealing half-rueful smile he had perfected for those businessmen whom he was wooing for his environmental causes. His cousins returned his smile. His aunt did not.

Imogene held Teddy's hand tightly letting everyone know that, no matter what was said, she'd stand by her man. Derita opened the drapes so she could see out, although there was little to see except the empty tennis court and a little of the lake.

Catherine chose a corner chair and tried to fade into the background. Charles scooted close to her and whispered, "Remember we used to call this library Queen Bess's throne room?"

Catherine nodded and whispered back. "From here, she ruled over her domain, meted out judgments, and kept reminding us of our fathers' failures. She was convinced none of us would amount to anything."

Charles grinned. "And I guess, in her estimation, she was right."

Bess cleared her throat. All whispering stopped and five faces turned in her direction.

"Now that everybody is here," she said, "we'll get started. I want to share with you what I've decided about my future and my holdings."

"So you've changed your will?" Teddy asked. His scowl resembled that of a bulldog who had lost his bone.

"Not exactly. Each of you will still get an equal share of whatever is left of my money when I die. Of course, I don't know how much that will be. You'll understand what I mean when I explain my circumstances."

Her words came easily and Charles risked one more whispered comment, "She must have taken a double dose of her asthma medicine. Not a single wheeze." Catherine nodded and Teddy gave his brother a dirty look.

Their aunt continued, "I'm getting rid of the Blue Goose and all my surrounding land." Bess waited until the gasping died down to finish her statement. "I'm moving away."

The cousins' words tumbled over each other. "Where are you going?"

"Why haven't you told us sooner?"

"What's going on?"

"Where does that leave us?"

A slight smile played on Bess's lips. It was as if Bess was enjoying her family's dismay and wanted to prolong their worry before striking the final blow. "In case you haven't noticed," Bess said, "the lodge is in need of painting and repairs; the yard is an eyesore; the pier is crumbling. The whole thing is a mess."

"Of course we've noticed," Teddy jumped in, "but we thought it was because you just didn't care."

"You're right about that. I don't care about the Blue Goose. I never have. It was Henry's pride and joy—not mine. I only kept it after his death because it was a good investment. Now it isn't."

Teddy slid his chair closer to Bess. "But it could be. Remember what Derita and I suggested to you?"

"Yes, I remember. At one time or another each one of you has told me what you want to happen to the Blue Goose after I'm gone. Well, I'm going, but not in the way you expected." Her speech became more difficult, her breaths shorter. "I think you all know that Charles wants a nature preserve, a noble vision perhaps, but not very practical. He has no idea where the money would come from to maintain it. I can't imagine people standing in line to buy tickets to see a few deer or raccoons or beavers." Imogene snickered while Charles slouched back in his chair.

"On the other hand," Bess said, "Teddy's scheme has some merit."

Charles straightened up and glared at Teddy and Imogene, both of whom sported wide grins. "And what kind of scheme is that?" Charles blurted out.

Bess went on before Teddy had a chance to answer. "It seems that Teddy has evolved into quite an entrepreneur. He wants to bring in developers: condos, beach cottages, water slides, the works. He thinks it will restore the Blue Goose to its former glory." Teddy took a slight bow and Charles shot him a look of disgust. Bess continued. "He's also convinced Derita to go along with him. While he's developing the land, she'll turn the lodge into a fat farm where her friends would pay good money to lose a few pounds."

Derita laughed. "Actually, Aunt Bess, I had in mind a luxury health and fitness spa. But you're right about my friends being willing to pay good money, especially with the right person running it."

"By 'right person' I assume you're referring to your latest fiancé. Frankly, I think you just want to set your next husband up in business."

"So what? Think of it as a dowry."

Bess gave a snort which ended in a coughing spell. When she was able, she went on, "Which brings us to Catherine's request." All the faces turned toward Catherine's corner. "She thinks I should sell out and give the money to medical research." Teddy's and Imogene's faces registered shock; Charles half-way nodded while Derita giggled. Catherine burrowed deeper into her chair.

"So, enough of this nonsense," Charles glared at his aunt. "What is going to happen?"

Bess took her time answering. The family waited. Finally the matriarch spoke. "It's going to be sold—to the highest bidder. As I said, Teddy's and Derita's ideas have merit, but I can't wait that long to get my money. I need it now to live on. The Blue Goose is not the only investment of mine which has lost its value—so have most of my others. The truth is, I'm nearly broke. I can't afford to keep up the lodge, I can't afford to finance any of your dreams or schemes, and I'm clearing out."

Catherine spoke for the first time since the meeting started. "But where will you go?"

"I've decided a lot of my breathing problems are due to the climate here: the humidity and the awful pollen from the woods. Dr. Caldwell thinks I should go to a nursing home. Such nonsense!" Bess tried to take a deep breath and failed. She compromised with several quick short breaths and kept talking. "Instead I've decided to move to Arizona." She waited a moment for that information to sink in, but before any of the others could make a comment, she went on, "Dr. Caldwell thinks I'm crazy, but then, he's thought that for years. I've contacted a doctor in Phoenix who thinks I could probably live several more years by making the move."

The cousins looked at each other and then back to their aunt. Derita finally broke the stunned silence. "That's wonderful, Aunt Bess. Arizona is beautiful. I'm sure you'll love it there."

"Yes," Catherine said. "It's great. You'll have a chance at a new life."

"Not many people get that," Imogene put in. "It's like a movie with a happy ending."

Teddy jumped up. "Yeah, yeah. That's great for you, but what's going to happen to us? What do you mean you're getting rid of the Blue Goose?" Imogene tugged at Teddy's hand but he ignored her. "And what about the risks? There's no guarantee the move will help you any and just the trip itself could be hazardous. And what if something happened to you way out there? You'd have no family around to help."

"In case you haven't noticed," Bess said dryly, "my family hasn't been around much the last few years anyway."

"Why, Aunt Bess," Imogene smiled as she succeeded in pulling her husband back to his seat. "You know Teddy and I made a special trip up to see you this spring. We all care very much about what happens to you."

Bess ignored Imogene's remarks. "As I was saying, I've gotten used to not having family around. I'll find a good housekeeper, maybe not as good as Lillian, but I'll find someone. And I'll hire nurses around the clock. You needn't worry about me; I'll be well cared for."

"Well, I'm all for it." Derita went over and gave her aunt a hug. "We'll all be rooting for you. Just let us know what we can do to help."

"Derita's right," Charles said. "And when you're feeling better, we'll all come out for a visit." Charles hesitated. "So do you have a buyer for the Blue Goose?"

"Yes. Like I said, it's going to the highest bidder. I need all the money I can get right now. Arizona and nurses and housekeepers don't come cheaply."

"You're exactly right," Teddy said. "Let me get in touch with the right developer and everything will be okay. You can have your money right away. I know the people who can make it happen."

"With you getting a good kickback, of course," Bess retorted. "And don't say 'okay.' You know I despise such slang. Furthermore, you can stop acting so innocent. You don't fool me, Teddy Faircloth. I know you've already been wheeling and dealing. Well, you can forget all that. I've made my own deal."

Five faces stared at the old woman as she tugged her afghan up closer to her chin and spat out her final words. "It so happens the highest bidder is a logging company. They'll clear-cut the land, demolish the lodge, and do whatever else they want to do. It won't matter to me. I won't be here."

"No!" Charles exploded. "You can't do that. It's outrageous. You'll ruin the entire area."

Derita shook her head. "It'll be such a shame to lose the lodge. It has such historic value. I remember Uncle Henry saying that even the governor used to come here to hunt."

"And hundreds would still come if they had some place to stay," Teddy said. "Developing the area would be an economic boost to the entire county. It would bring in tourists and money and prestige. That's what's needed around here. You can't destroy this place on a whim."

Imogene nodded vigorously and opened her mouth to say something, but Bess didn't give her a chance. "It's not a whim," Bess said, facing her family with grim determination. "It's a good business decision—the only good one I've made lately. The logging company wanted just to buy the lumber and leave the land, but I insisted if they wanted the trees they'd have to buy everything. They agreed, and at my price."

Derita clenched the arms of her chair, but kept her voice calm. "Have you talked to Jake about this yet? He's lived here all his life. He loves the lake, the area, the beauty."

"Yes, I told Jake," Bess said, "and he's furious with me. Says it will ruin the view for the other lake people. But I can't worry about other people. I have to do what's best for me."

"Of course it'll ruin the view. It'll ruin Lake Lucia for everybody," Teddy cried. "Imagine looking out from your front porch and seeing a denuded hillside with nothing but stumps left. It's unthinkable."

Charles pushed back his chair and stepped toward his aunt. "You can't do this! I won't let you. I'll stop you some way—somehow!"

"Oh, do sit down, Charles," Derita said in a mocking voice. "Your melodramatics aren't going to help any. It's apparent Aunt Bess has given this a lot of thought." She smiled at her aunt. "We'll just have to make the best of it."

From the sanctuary of her corner, Catherine spoke softly, "But why, Aunt Bess? Why would you want to sell out to loggers? It doesn't make sense."

Bess looked in that direction. The afternoon sun was fading and Catherine was nearly hidden in the shadow. "But that's what you said you wanted," Bess gave Catherine a frozen smile. "You suggested I sell the lodge and give the money for medical research. So I'm selling. Only the money is going to treat my disease—not yours."

Catherine stood up. "If it's living expenses you need you can have the stock Uncle Henry left me. I've never done anything with it. The money will never do me any good anyway."

"And I can help you out some," Charles said.

"The trees are more important to me than any amount of money."

Bess shook her head. "I don't need anybody's help. I never have and I never will."

Charles threw up his hands, started from the room and then looked back. "Is there anything we can say to change your mind?"

"Nothing. I've made my decision."

Teddy stared after his departing brother and then looked helplessly at his cousins. Derita shrugged, Catherine studied the faded carpet. Imogene tugged at her husband's arm and whispered in his ear. Teddy nodded at her and approached Bess. "Surely you haven't signed anything yet," he said. "Have you?"

Bess gave a sigh and shook her head. "I have an appointment in the morning with the buyer and my lawyer. It'll all be settled then." She dropped her head in fatigue. "I'm going to my room to rest a bit. I'll see all of you at dinner." Derita jumped up to help Bess from her chair, but her aunt waved her away. "Tell Lillian I've invited Jake to dinner also."

FOUR

DINNER WAS A SOMBER AFFAIR. The children were bubbling over in excitement to tell of their afternoon in and on the water, but their enthusiasm didn't touch the adults. Allison noted that Charles seemed too distracted to listen, Teddy sullen, Imogene worried, and Derita bored. Catherine kept looking out the window like a prisoner planning an escape, and Bess seemed too tired to care.

It was obvious to Allison the future of the Blue Goose occupied their minds, but they didn't want to discuss it, at least, not in front of their aunt.

Allison, seated between Jake and Imogene with the silence beginning to smother her, decided the weather might be a good place to start small talk with the old man. He agreed that the last few days had been lovely. "But that dry spell in May hurt my peach trees," he said. "Got scale insects. Pesky things. They can ruin the trees if you're not careful. Had to buy spray to poison them. Expensive stuff but worth it." Allison nodded her head in agreement although she knew nothing about fruit trees, and bug spray was not exactly what she considered good table conversation. Jake must have thought otherwise. "Yep. I got enough poison to kill every bad bug in the county and then some. You know what I mean? But I take care of my peaches. There's nothing like chomping down on a ripe, juicy Elberta."

"You're right about that," Allison said. "I remember my grandmother had a tree in her back yard. We kids would eat them right off the tree, not even bother to wash them. The juice would run down our chins, stain our clothes, even get in our hair. But it was a taste right out of heaven."

Jake gave her a gap-tooth grin. He smeared butter on a hot biscuit, but took only a small nibble. He shook his head sadly. "Those days are gone forever. Can't eat fruit off trees anymore. Probably kill you if you did. I don't like using the spray, you understand. But it's either that or lose my trees." His eyes flickered to the head of the table where Bess struggled for breath between bites. Allison studied the old man. His face and eyes reminded her of a worried basset hound. His plaid flannel shirt looked like it had been worn summer and winter for more years than she liked to contemplate. His only concession to the warm evening was to roll up the sleeves, which revealed bony arms covered with stringy gray hair. His left hand clenched the uneaten biscuit, crumbling it to minute pieces. "Life is full of hard choices," he whispered. "You know what I mean?"

"I guess," Allison faltered, waiting for Jake to elaborate. But he didn't. Instead he looked in dismay at his butter-coated hand, then carefully wiped it with his napkin. Allison glanced around the table.

There was little hope of a conversation with any of the others: the cousins were picking at their food, the children were asking for seconds, Imogene was whispering to her husband. Allison took another chance with the old man. "I take it you've lived around here a long time?"

Jake bobbed his head. "Most of my life. The lake is not only my home, it's my friend." He gave Allison a quick smile. "You might say it's my sweetheart since I never married. Bess even accuses me of making it my religion. I can sit on the shore and become one with the water. On calm days the water reflects peace, the stillness of the soul. And on stormy days I can feel the energy of the universe, the cleansing of detritus from the bottom of my life."

Allison gaped in astonishment at the poetry spilling out of the mouth of this shriveled Methuselah. Jake suddenly seemed embarrassed. "Sorry. I can't talk that way to many people. Somehow I thought you'd understand."

"But I do. Really I do. I love the water too." Allison squirmed nervously. "In fact, I consider lakes and oceans a source of healing power." She smiled. "I can't say that to many people either. I guess we have something in common."

"Looks like." The old man again turned his eyes to the head of the table. "I knew Bess didn't like the lake, but I never imagined she would desecrate it." He turned back to face Allison. "She's got to be stopped, you know." He wiped his mouth and pushed back from the table. "Excuse me. I need to take a little walk. It was nice meeting you." Before Allison could say anything else, Jake was gone. No one else appeared to notice his departure.

Allison turned to her other side. Lillian had brought in more sweet-potato casserole and insisted Teddy have another serving. He smiled at her and obliged. Imogene, on the other hand, ignored her potatoes and ate her English peas one at a time. Maybe I can start a conversation with Katherine Hepburn, Allison thought. "I understand you're an actress," she said when she had caught Imogene's attention. "That must be fascinating."

Imogene came alive as if a spotlight had just enveloped her. "Oh, yes. It's such a thrill to be on stage. Have you ever acted?"

Allison shook her head. "No. I'd probably get stage fright so badly I wouldn't even remember my name—or the name of whomever I was supposed to be."

"Oh, it's such fun. Every eye on you, people waiting for you to make them laugh or cry, or get scared. It's quite a responsibility." Imogene gave up even the pretense of eating now that she had an audience. "I do all kinds of roles. I just finished playing in *The Fabulous Franklins*. It's about three generations of a Southern family. I aged from a young girl to a grandmother. I had to change not only my appearance, but mannerisms, voice, posture. Very challenging."

"I'm sure it was," Allison agreed.

"I can do any part. I've played an angel, a school

teacher, the girlfriend of a death-row inmate, even a hooker." Imogene paused and a scowl crossed her face. "Of course, it's amateur theater, but I plan to go professional soon."

"Well, you certainly are versatile," Allison said trying to inject a note of admiration in her voice, while fervently hoping one of the other dinner guests would direct a scrap of conversation her way. It didn't happen. "I guess your acting career doesn't leave you much time for anything else."

"Just my jewelry designs. I design all my own jewelry." Imogene shook a heavy silver bracelet in front of Allison. "What do you think?"

"It's beautiful. You actually designed it?" Allison was beginning to feel like she must be talking to the winner of a Miss USA talent contest. "Then you *make* the jewelry too?" It seemed like the next sensible question.

Imogene laughed. "Oh, no. That process is a little complicated. There's a company in Charlotte that makes the pieces for me. They give me free rein in the plant, though, so I can watch each step as they do it. It's very interesting."

"I'm sure it is." Jewelry had never been a factor in Allison's life. She had tossed her wedding band years ago after her husband had split—and one doesn't wear dangling bracelets while shooting baskets. She wondered if she should regale Imogene with stories of her exciting life in school locker rooms.

Luckily, Catherine made that unnecessary as she

stood up. "I could use some fresh air. How about you, Allison?" They excused themselves and stepped out to the front porch.

"I think I hear Paul's pontoon coming around," Allison said. "You'd better get down to the dock, Cat. He wants to take you for a ride."

"All right," Catherine said, "but you're coming with us." She grabbed Allison by the hand and jogged down the hill. Allison tried to protest, but Catherine would have none of it. "I'm not going out on that lake alone with a handsome stranger. For all we know he might be a mass murderer looking for his next victim."

Allison sighed. The soft June night was made for romance, the kind of night Allison had nearly forgotten ever existed. "Cat, you're impossible. If I were ten years younger, I'd scratch your eyes out for a chance at him."

Paul pulled the pontoon expertly alongside the dock and held it steady while Allison and Catherine boarded. He greeted them with a smile worthy of a Disney World charmer. "Welcome aboard, ladies, to the USS Daggert and a magical moonlight cruise on Lake Lucia."

After they had cleared the channel, Paul shifted the motor down to a slower speed and a lower octave. "That's better," he said. "Now we can talk without shouting."

"And you can start," Catherine said with a big smile, "by telling us all about yourself, Paul. Since you told my cousin I could vouch for your character, I think you'd better tell me what I'm vouching for."

Allison jumped in. She'd learned long ago that if you want to find out something, you need to ask. "So, where do you come from? Why are you here? And what are your plans for the future?"

Paul laughed. "Sounds like my last job interview." He gave them a sure-fire, confident, *I'm your man,* smile.

"And what kind of job was that?" Allison asked.

"Associate minister. Archdale Community Church."

Allison's mouth dropped open. She could have imagined a salesman, an airline pilot, even an insurance agent. But a minister? "How interesting," she said. "Isn't that interesting, Cat?"

"Yes, I find that very interesting." For some reason Catherine seemed to be trying not to grin.

Allison studied the two people in front of her and befitting her possible role as a matchmaker, she asked the all-important question. "And what does your wife think about it?"

Paul's gaze didn't flinch. "She *did* think it was interesting." Allison caught the emphasis on "did" and waited for his next words. "My wife was killed in an accident two years ago." Allison heard the tremor in his voice. She slid closer to him, reached out and placed her hand over his. "I'm sorry. It must have been so hard." It was a simple gesture from one person who understood pain to another who had also suffered.

Paul carefully steered the pontoon around a small boat bearing a lone twilight fisherman, before he answered. "Yes. But with God's help, I've made it through." His face and voice revealed no bitterness. The pain had been dealt with and accepted.

Catherine turned puzzled eyes to the captain of the craft. "I guess being a minister must have helped," she said. "After all, clergymen are supposed to be on speaking terms with God. But somehow I never thought that privilege applied to ordinary people."

Paul frowned. "Now that's an opening for a sermon if I ever heard one."

Catherine held up her hands in mock protest. "Not tonight. I get enough sermons from my aunt. So let's change the subject. How did you come to be her next door neighbor?"

"Just lucky, I guess." Paul's quick wit and engaging smile returned. "Actually what happened was that Fate gave me two choices for my vacation: I could go to Carowinds and get sick on all the rides or I could go camping on a little known lake and meet two charming, intelligent schoolmarms. I'm glad I chose the latter."

Catherine giggled a little, more like a schoolgirl than a schoolmarm. "How did you know we were teachers?"

"Allison filled me in while you were at the family gathering."

"I'm afraid to ask what else she told you," Catherine said.

"Not much. But I have a whole week to find out more."

Allison watched the two of them like a proud gym teacher watching her clumsy students learn to dribble basketballs. The pontoon was slowly circling the lake in the dimming light. The sun had disappeared, the moon just barely in sight. A slight breeze had arisen, but it held no chill. The boat's occupants were in no hurry for the trip to end.

"You know," Paul went on, "I was thinking this might be a great place to bring my youth group camping later in the summer. They'd love it here."

"You might as well scratch that idea," Catherine said. "No one is going to love it here if Aunt Bess gets away with her diabolical plan."

"What do you mean?" Paul asked.

"I guess there's no reason not to tell you. It'll be public information after tomorrow."

Catherine again related the gist of the family meeting but left out some of the details she had revealed to Allison.

"I guess that's what is known as good news-bad news," Paul said. "It's good that your aunt has a chance for better health, but it's terrible that it has to be financed by sacrificing the lodge and the land."

"That's what so hard to understand. I don't believe it has to be that way. I'm positive Aunt Bess has more money than she's admitting to. She doesn't have to sell out to loggers to finance her move to Arizona."

"Then why?" Allison asked. She knew the answer

wasn't any of her business and for a moment she worried that Catherine would tell her so. Instead Catherine shook her head. "I guess she has her reasons."

A comfortable silence settled over the three as the boat eased its way through the still water. Catherine peered through the darkness back to the lodge. Finally she said, "I guess we'd better be heading back. Looks like almost everybody else has turned in for the night."

Most of the lodge stood in darkness. Allison could see lights in Derita's room, but none in Bess's room. The only light on the ground floor came from the billiard room. She wondered if the brothers were having a late night game.

"All right," Paul said as he turned the boat toward shore. The water began to shimmer under the moon's spell like tinsel on a Christmas tree, and stars began to blink their way out to an all-night party. "It's a shame to leave all this, but I wouldn't want you to get locked out."

"No chance of that," Catherine said. "No one around here locks doors. I doubt if the lodge's doors have been locked in thirty years."

Allison let out a low groan. "I wished you hadn't told me that, Cat. Personally, I like locked doors."

Paul slowed the motor to a purr. "I can't help thinking of what your aunt plans to do to this beautiful lake. Like Allison, I have to wonder why she would do such a thing."

Catherine shrugged. "Aunt Bess never really

seemed to like the Blue Goose. It was Uncle Henry's dream and delight, not hers. She went along with it because it was good business. She stayed after his death because it was still good business to do so. Now she has a chance to rid herself of it completely and make a huge profit. She doesn't have a sentimental bone in her body, and it doesn't matter to her whom she hurts."

The pontoon swung around by the dock. "Well, we have a few more days to enjoy it anyway," Paul said cheerfully. "And to get better acquainted. How about meeting me for a morning swim?" He was talking to Catherine, but seemed to suddenly remember his manners, "You too, Allison?"

Allison knew when to refuse an invitation. "Thanks, but I think I'll stick to my morning run."

"The swim sounds good to me," Catherine replied. "About sevenish?"

Paul grinned. "I said morning, not predawn. Let's try for eight."

THE LODGE WAS DARK when Catherine and Allison made their way around to the back door. Lancelot lay in wait for them. As Catherine reached to open the screen door, the cat maneuvered his way between her legs, ready to scoot inside. Allison thwarted his plan. "Not this time, Lancelot," Allison said, as she gently picked up the cat and placed him by his feeding dish. "Finish your supper now, and keep the night creatures away."

When they reached the top of the stairs Catherine

said, "Let's check on the kids before turning in." She quietly cracked open the door of the end room assigned to Becky. Slivers of moonlight danced over the slumbering girl. Catherine stepped into the room and stood by the bedside. The wild tomboy had disappeared and in her place lay a lovely sleeping princess. Bending over, Catherine kissed the child's smooth forehead, tucked in an exposed arm and said what sounded to Allison like a prayer, "Please let her have a happy life."

Across the hall was Wesley's room. Allison waited outside the door as Catherine slipped into the room. A whisper squeaked through the darkness, "Is that you, Dad?"

"No. It's Catherine. Just checking on you, Tiger. Thought you'd be sleeping by now."

"I can't sleep. Will you stay with me for a while?"

Catherine inched her way toward the bed. "Sure, I'll stay a little bit. Would you like me to find a night light to put in here? It's mighty dark on this side of the house."

"No. I'm not afraid of the dark." Wesley reached out for Catherine's hand. "It's the voices."

"Voices? What voices? Everything's quiet in here." Catherine sat on the boy's bed and Allison tried to make out his face. She could see only a white sheet pulled tautly under his chin and thin arms over the cover.

"Not in here. Out there." The boy's arm pointed to the open window. He whispered, "I think they're in the cemetery."

Catherine chuckled. "So your dad's been telling you ghost stories about the old cemetery? He used to love to scare Derita and me with his spooky tales. Don't pay any attention to him. He's just teasing you."

"It's not that, Catherine. They were real voices. I heard them. They were coming from beyond the tennis court. I looked out the window, but I couldn't see anybody. But I heard them. Honest I did."

Allison was glad Wesley couldn't see her smiling in the shadows. Kids had such wild imaginations and he was so serious about this. "And what did the voices say?" Catherine asked.

"I don't know. I couldn't hear that good. But I know they were men—maybe bad men."

"You should have told your dad. He'd have gotten up and chased them away." Allison knew Catherine was trying her best to act as if she believed the boy.

"I wanted to, but he's not in his room. He said he was going to bed when he tucked me in, but he didn't. I don't know where he is."

That's strange, Allison thought. She hadn't noticed any lights in the downstairs rooms and hadn't seen anybody when she and Catherine came up from the lake. Even the light in the billiard room was out when they came in.

"Well, I don't hear anything now," Catherine assured Wesley. "They're probably gone. You try to get some sleep and, if you like, you can go swimming with Paul and me in the morning."

Wesley turned on his side. "I'd like that. But will you leave my door open a little, so I can hear Daddy when he comes in?"

FIVE

ALLISON WAS AN EARLY RISER even when school was not in session. She woke with the first hesitant rays of sunlight, jumped into her jogging suit and shoes, and headed out her door. She heard no one else stirring as she tiptoed quietly down the stairs. On her way down Allison nearly tripped over Lancelot dozing peacefully on the bottom step. She scooped the cat up in her arms and carried him outdoors. "How in the world did you get into the house? Are you one of those mythical creatures who ooze through closed doors, do magical tricks, and read people's minds? If so, then you know I'm thinking right now that you are an absolute nuisance." Lancelot didn't take kindly to Allison's remonstrances, leapt from her arms, and ran up the drive. "All right, go then. I can't be bothered with you anyway."

Not knowing much about the lay of the land, Allison wasn't sure where the best place to run would be. She remembered seeing Teddy and Imogene heading toward the woods yesterday and decided there must be a good path. She couldn't imagine Imogene fighting underbrush to get close to nature.

Just behind the garage, Allison found an opening into the woods. She ran cautiously until the path became wider and smoother, then she was able to speed up to her usual jogging pace. Her delight in finding such a running space was clouded by increasing uneasiness. The path showed evidence of recent maintenance. The weeds were cut, branches were trimmed out of the way, and the occasional raw dirt revealed multiple footprints. How strange, Allison thought, considering the neglected front yard yesterday.

She began to wonder about the wisdom of continuing her run. Some of those footprints looked like they had been freshly made. There was no legal hunting season this time of year and she had seen *No Trespassing* signs posted along the driveway. Why would anybody be tramping about in the woods? Allison stopped abruptly. In front of her, intersecting with the path, she saw a road—a newly constructed road. It consisted of only two large ruts, but it was smooth enough and wide enough for trucks. In fact, she could make out the tracks of cleated tires. The road disappeared over a slight rise. She couldn't see or hear anything, but she sensed something was terribly wrong. Catherine had indicated that the woods were used only by hunters, and Teddy hadn't mentioned seeing anything unusual last evening. Surely he and Imogene must have seen this during their walk.

As she continued to look around, Allison spied in the distance what looked like little yellow flags on sticks stuck into the ground. She went closer to investigate. The flags were planted at intervals on both sides of the road. They seemed to be outlining specific areas. It's almost as if someone was laying out a subdivision, she thought. But that's impossible. Catherine had said that her aunt had made it very clear what she intended to do with the land. Then she remembered something else Catherine had quoted her aunt as saying, something about Teddy already wheeling and dealing. Maybe this is what Bess suspected. Allison yanked one of the flags out of the ground and slid it under her sweat shirt. "I have to tell Catherine about this," she muttered.

ALLISON ARRIVED BACK at the lodge expecting a substantial breakfast and interesting conversation. What she found was ominous silence: no one in the kitchen, or the dining room, or the library. Surely, she thought, they can't all still be sleeping.

She turned to go up the stairs when she heard a knock on the back door. Through the screen she could see Paul. He was wearing swim trunks, a tee shirt, and a concerned frown. "I'm looking for Catherine. She didn't show up for our swim date."

"I'm looking for her too. There doesn't seem to be anybody around." Allison motioned him to come in. "Let's check upstairs."

As they topped the stair landing, Allison heard a murmur of voices and saw the house occupants gathered at the far end of the hall. Catherine looked up, noticed the two of them, and met them halfway.

Without any preliminaries, she said, "Aunt Bess is dead."

Allison gasped, "But when? How?"

Paul didn't say a word. He reached out his arms to his new-found friend and, without shrinking back, Catherine accepted his comforting embrace.

Derita approached them. "Dr. Caldwell said for us to wait in the library. He'll be down in a few minutes."

Allison watched the cousins as they drooped by. Her impressions were not kind. Derita was already in full makeup, wore a fawn-colored pant suit and gold earrings which nearly touched her shoulders. Imogene clung to Teddy's arm, but it was hard to tell who was supporting whom. Teddy's face was blank while Imogene assumed a perfect mourning appearance: lips curved downwards, slightly smeared mascara, and an occasional sniff as she tried to keep back tears. Charles had an arm around each of his children in an effort to comfort them, but his face seemed to hold a look of triumph. Becky and Wesley looked bewildered. They probably hadn't known their great-aunt well enough to be devastated by her death, but at their age, any death was a threat to their safe little world. Looking at Catherine, Allison couldn't decide what she was seeing: grief or relief?

When they reached the top of the stairs, Allison said, "You go on down, Cat. Paul and I will wait. We don't want to intrude at a time like this." Catherine nodded and joined the rest of the family. Then Allison saw another figure coming toward them.

"That must be Serena," Allison told Paul. "She comes in to serve breakfast. Maybe she can tell us something." Allison didn't want to appear to be prying, but she did want to know some details.

Serena was delighted to find another audience. "Like I told the others, I came in as usual and fixed a tray for Mrs. L. She likes her breakfast at seven-thirty sharp. I don't dare be late or she'll start talking about how this younger generation is careless and lazy. I knocked on the door like I always do, but I never wait for an answer. She always told me just to come on in, that she wasn't going to waste any breath to tell me to come in. So that's what I did." Serena stopped talking long enough to take a deep breath and Allison studied her informant. Allison took the girl to be in her twenties, a little overweight, and out of shape. She had a pretty face, little makeup, curly red hair which probably became kinky in damp weather, scattered freckles, and honest green eyes. Allison liked her.

"Well, like I said," Serena went on, "I went in and put the tray on her bedside table and I said, 'Good morning,' like I always do, and then she usually grunts and sits up. But this morning she didn't move. So I said louder, 'Good morning, Mrs. L., I've got your oatmeal here.' She alternates between oatmeal and bran flakes. This was her oatmeal morning. But still she never moved, never grunted—nothing. It was then I really looked at her. Her right arm was dangling off the bed and her mouth was open like she'd been surprised. Now I haven't seen much in this world, but I know dead when I see it. And Mrs. L. was it."

Paul had been listening carefully to every word. When Serena paused, he asked kindly, "And what did you do then?"

"Went over to wake up Derita and tell her. But I sure was wishing the nurse was here to handle the problem. I always figured Derita was too pretty to have much sense. But I guess I was wrong. She was just as calm as could be. Came over to check her aunt out for herself and agreed with me that Mrs. L. was dead. Then Derita politely asked me to tell the others while she called the doctor. So I knocked on the cousins' doors and told them. They all came out, but Derita wouldn't let any of them in the room. She said they had to wait for the doctor to get here."

"Did they wait?" Allison asked.

"Sure did. I went back in, though," Serena continued. "I figured I'd better clean up in there a little bit while we were waiting."

Paul frowned. "Clean what up?"

"Her medicine bottles. They were scattered on the floor and under the bed. I guess she must have had a bad spell and knocked over her pills trying to get to them." Serena shrugged her shoulders. "That's all I know. Dr. Caldwell is still in there. Wonder what's taking him so long." Serena started down the stairs. "I guess I'd better make some coffee for everybody."

Allison and Paul turned to leave when Dr. Caldwell came into the hall. He looked exactly like a family doctor should look: old, gray, wise. Allison had the impression that he was a good listener, a good comforter, but one who would not put up with any nonsense. Forgetting her statement about not wanting to intrude, she waited until he came up to her and then introduced herself and Paul. "We're friends of Catherine and want to do anything we can to help."

"Good. Then come with me while I tell the family the bad news."

Allison gave the doctor a puzzled look and said hesitantly, "But, Sir, they already know she's dead."

Dr. Caldwell nodded. "But what they don't know," he said, "is that she may have been murdered."

SIX

ONCE ALL THE COUSINS had their eyes focused on Dr. Caldwell, Allison and Paul slipped, unnoticed, into the library. Serena must have called Lillian. The housekeeper was sitting next to Bess's empty recliner alternately wiping her eyes and blowing her nose. She's the only one in the room who seems to be genuinely grieving, Allison thought. Then she revised that thought when Jake stumbled into the room. "I can't believe my Bess is gone," he sobbed. "Bess is gone." His voice trailed off into a low moan. "Gone."

Dr. Caldwell cleared his throat. "I can't determine Mrs. Lattimer's cause of death at the present time. Considering her illness, I might have expected her to expire from a respiratory crisis a few years from now or even in a few months, but I didn't expect it this soon. Her respiratory problems were quite well controlled with medication. She was even planning a trip to Arizona, although I didn't particularly approve of it." The doctor paused, brushed back his thinning gray hair, and his gaze went from one cousin to another. They waited impatiently. Allison found a chair next to Catherine and patted her hand in a gesture of comfort. Catherine pulled her hand away. "Why doesn't he just get this over with?" she muttered. "We've got a funeral to plan and then I'm out of here. I don't care what happens to the Blue Goose. I just want to put it behind me."

Allison wondered if the doctor was going to use the M word. "Since there is no clear cause of death," Dr. Caldwell went on, "I'm going to order an autopsy. Furthermore, I request that nobody enter Mrs. Lattimer's room, so nothing can be disturbed, until the police finish their investigation."

"Police?" "Autopsy?" "Investigation?" The words exploded from every direction.

Teddy vaulted from his chair. "Are you crazy, Doc? Aunt Bess simply died. She was sick and she died. That's all there is to it."

"This is really ridiculous, Dr. Caldwell," Derita said. "Surely there's no need for the police. You're making a big fuss over nothing. We all know how sick Aunt Bess was."

Charles's famous smile put in an appearance. "We certainly understand your professional caution, doctor. I assure you we'll cooperate in every way."

"Well, I'm not going to cooperate," Teddy said. "Imogene and I are going into that room and pay our respects to Aunt Bess. And you can't stop us."

"I can and I will." Dr. Caldwell was no longer the gentle, soft-spoken family physician. "I called the sheriff's department before I left your aunt's room. I believe I hear them driving up now."

Allison observed that Catherine sat stone-faced

after the doctor mentioned an autopsy. Wesley slid away from his father and crawled up close to Catherine. "What's happening? Why are the police coming?" Catherine gave him a reassuring smile and patted his knee, but didn't say a word.

Behind them Jake started sobbing again. "I'll miss you, Bess. I'll miss you." He sniffed loudly and covered his face with his gaunt, garden-stained hands. Allison tried to reconcile the apparently grief-stricken old man with the one who had said only yesterday that Bess had to be stopped from desecrating the lake. Well, somebody had stopped her. Had his love for the lake overridden his love of an old friend? Or was his anguish genuine?

Lillian went over to him and patted him on the back. Jake lifted his head and looked around the room. "None of them care, Lillian. They don't care."

Lillian shook her head. "I know. Nobody loved Bess like we did. They didn't understand her. They didn't try." She took Jake by his hand. "Come on out to the kitchen with me."

Allison regarded the two as they left the library. What virtues had they seen in Bess, she wondered, that everyone else had missed?

Paul touched Allison's hand to get her attention and whispered, "I'm going to run down to my trailer and get dressed. Tell Catherine I'll be back later." He left by the front door as the police were coming in the back.

DETECTIVE FRED SAWYER entered the library quietly and politely. Since the day was still young and the heat index in the friendly range, his navy-blue suit was unrumpled, his shirt crisp, his tie tightly knotted. He smiled at the gathered clan. He knew the importance of gaining the good will and confidence of family members. He also knew that Bess Lattimer had not been especially well liked around Lake Lucia or in the nearby county seat, but she *had* been respected. She had money and influence, and that goes a long way in small towns. Fred had seen the cousins from time to time through the years, but he'd had no particular dealings with them. However, he knew Lillian, Serena, and Jake quite well.

Fred introduced himself and his assistant, Gail Jordan, to the cousins and their guest. Gail, in turn, carefully wrote each of their names in her small notebook. She had been working with Fred only for a year, but she'd become invaluable to him during investigations. He did the questioning, she did the paperwork. He admired her efficiency and her professionalism. She wore her African heritage proudly, being tall and slim and dark and regal. He was just the opposite: short, a little portly, a very ordinary face inherited from his English ancestors. Fred knew they made a rather odd combination, but that was all right, they got the job done. Their respect for each other, although often cloaked by light banter, was real.

"We're here at Dr. Caldwell's request," Fred explained. "Mrs. Lattimer's death was sudden and unexpected, and therefore has to be investigated."

Charles nodded his head. "Of course, we understand you have to follow procedure," he said, "but surely you don't think her death was anything except natural."

"I don't know. That's what we're here to find out. Usually a detective wouldn't be called in until after a preliminary investigation. But I was in the office when Dr. Caldwell called and since I've known Dick Caldwell for years, I respect his suspicions."

"Suspicions of what?" Teddy stood up and took a step toward Fred.

Fred shrugged. "I told you that's what we're here to find out. Now you people make yourselves comfortable. Miss Jordan and I are going to look at the scene and will be back later to talk to you."

Dr. Caldwell led the way to the stairs, followed by the detectives. Allison joined them. At the top step all three turned and looked at her questioningly. "I just want to tell you something," Allison stammered.

"And what is that?" Fred asked. He recalled that Allison had been introduced simply as Catherine's friend. He wondered how she would know anything relevant to the case, if indeed there was a case.

"Dr. Caldwell said he didn't want the room disturbed," Allison said, "but it had already been disturbed before he arrived." She had their complete attention. "It probably isn't important, but Serena told me that while they waited for the doctor, she picked up medicine bottles that were strewn on the floor. I thought you would want to talk to her about it."

"Thank you. We'll do just that." This gal is sharp,

Fred thought. She might turn out to be of some help—if she doesn't get in the way.

Gail turned to the doctor, notebook in hand. "Did Serena say anything to you about the medicines?"

"No. But then I didn't ask her anything," Dr. Caldwell answered. "Thought I'd leave all that up to the proper authorities."

Allison backed away. "Well, I thought you ought to know. I'll be downstairs if you need me."

ALLISON FELT thoroughly rebuked. I was just trying to help, she told herself. Before going back downstairs, she went to her room to change into more appropriate clothes. As she pulled off her sweat shirt, a small yellow flag fluttered to the floor. She picked it up and tossed it on the dresser. I have no idea what these things were doing in the woods, she thought, but I don't have time to think about it now.

When she returned to the library, Serena was pouring fresh coffee and Lillian had brought in a plate of cinnamon rolls. She was coaxing Teddy to have one. Teddy humored her with a sad smile and reached for one. Imogene shook her head. Derita was on the phone in the corner, Charles had taken the children outside where they were busily kicking a soccer ball around, and Catherine was nowhere in sight.

Allison moved to the window and looked out to the lake. She saw Catherine on the pier staring toward the brush where Paul was emerging. He motioned her to the yard swing. Allison decided

Catherine was in good hands and turned her thoughts back to the present situation.

She silently reviewed the few facts she knew: Bess Lattimer was dead, the doctor thought it was murder, and if so, everyone in the house would be suspect. Allison always liked to think the best of people; it was hard for her to imagine anyone here as a murderer. But from what Catherine had told her about the family meeting yesterday, there were plenty of motives. If Bess died before signing a sales agreement, the lodge and the land would be saved from loggers. Was that important enough to kill for?

Allison had read enough mysteries to know the detectives always looked for motive, means, and opportunity. The means was still unknown, but there was probably ample opportunity for any one of the suspects to enter Bess's bedroom and do whatever it was he or she did. Allison shook her head. I need a cup of coffee, she thought, and I need to leave the detective work to the proper authorities as the good doctor suggested.

The coffee pot had disappeared from the library, so Allison wandered out to the kitchen, helped herself to the biggest mug she could find, and filled it to the brim. She never used cream or sugar. It was the caffeine her body and mind craved. She also craved something chocolate. Cinnamon rolls just didn't cut it with her. A search of the kitchen, though, revealed only a few crumbs of chocolate chip cookies. Giving up her search, Allison returned to the library.

The detective was hunkered down at one end of the couch while Derita perched at the other end. His assistant sat at the desk with her notebook open. In her mind, Allison was already referring to them as Fred and Gail. She had taken an almost instant liking to them and was sure it wouldn't be long before they were on a first name basis.

All the others had left the room. Allison slithered into a corner chair and unabashedly listened to the conversation.

"Father and mother will be flying in tomorrow," Derita explained to Fred. "They'll be here for the funeral."

Fred nodded. "That's fine. Now you understand we just want to get some general information. This isn't a formal interrogation. There'll be some other officers and the medical examiner here shortly to go over the room, gather evidence, photograph and secure the scene. Then we'll wait for the medical examiner's report. But it would be helpful if you could briefly tell us the events of last evening and this morning."

"Sure," Derita said. "I'm glad to help all I can." She took both hands and flipped her hair back, adjusted the rings on her right hand, and smiled demurely. "Aunt Bess was tired and went to her room right after dinner."

"What time was that?" Gail asked, her pen poised for action.

"Some time after seven. I carried her some fresh water. She said she was going to read awhile and then would take her bedtime medications. She shooed me out of the room. Said she was fine."

"And what did you do?" Fred asked.

"I came back downstairs. Everyone else had gone outside, but I didn't much feel like talking to anybody, so I watched a little TV in here. There wasn't anything good on, so I found a book, read about an hour, and then went up and took my shower. When I was drying off, I thought I heard a noise from Aunt Bess's room. The bathroom is located between our rooms."

"Yes, we know," Gail said.

Derita flinched but made no comment. She went on with her account. "I opened the bathroom door slightly and asked if she was all right. She answered that she was okay, and for me to leave her alone. I then said that the night air was getting cool and that I would come in and close her window when I got my pajamas on. She didn't answer."

"Did you?" Fred asked.

"Did I what?"

"Did you go in and close the window?"

"Yes, that is, I went in, but the window was already closed. She must have gotten up and closed it herself. She was sleeping quietly so I went back to my room and went to bed."

Gail had been busy taking notes. "So we know she was alive when you spoke to her from the bathroom. And what time was that?"

"Probably close to nine-thirty."

"And then what happened this morning?" Gail asked as she turned a page in the notebook.

"Serena barged into my room, shook me awake, and said that Aunt Bess was dead."

Fred sipped his fast cooling coffee and asked, "Do you remember her exact words?"

"Well, let me see," Derita looked up to the ceiling for a few seconds and then said, "Her exact words were, 'You better wake up. Mrs. L. is dead.'"

"And then," Gail prompted.

"And then I got up, followed Serena back to Aunt Bess's room, realized she was right, and instructed her to tell the others while I called Dr. Caldwell."

"You called from your aunt's room?" Gail questioned.

"Yes. It's the only room upstairs that has a phone. Then I waited outside in the hall for the others. We all waited there until the doctor arrived."

"None of your cousins went into the room?" Fred asked.

"Teddy wanted to, but Imogene stopped him. I guess she thought it would be too much of a shock for him. Charles was busy trying to explain what had happened to the children and Catherine just stood there."

"So if all of you just stood around in the hall, when did everybody get dressed?"

Derita bit her lip. "Well, actually I did excuse myself to get dressed. I went into my room by the hall door. I didn't want to greet the doctor in my pajamas. I think all the others were already dressed. They're earlier risers than I am." Derita paused. "No, Catherine wasn't dressed. She had on a swim suit and a terry robe. She must have changed when I did because when I came back out she had on jeans."

Gail was scribbling furiously. Allison noticed Fred's smile as he glanced at his assistant. He probably used to do the same thing when he was new on the force, she thought. Now he seemed glad to let others take the notes which he could review at his leisure. At the same time, Allison was sure he was writing everything on his brain.

Fred told Derita she could be excused. Before seeking out the next cousin, Fred turned to Allison with an amused smile. "Did you get all that?"

Allison blushed. "You knew I was here all the time?"

"Sure. After all, we need all the help we can get. Any comments?"

"Actually yes. There was one question you forgot to ask."

Fred looked startled. "And that was?"

"Where did Derita put on her makeup? If it was in the bathroom, she could easily have slipped into Bess's room without being seen by the others."

"And why would she have done that?"

"I don't know. You're the detective."

Allison smiled at the country cop. He wasn't much to look at, she thought, but he spoke as one whose pockets were crammed with confidence. His eyes were strong, a little sad, the color of faded blue jeans. He looked like he'd ridden his share of motorcycles as well as sway-back horses, and she was sure he'd walked many lonely roads.

Her musings were interrupted when Teddy and Imogene wandered in from the kitchen. Allison could tell Teddy wasn't going to go hungry no matter what else happened at the Blue Goose. Imogene tugged at Teddy's arm. "The detective wants to talk to us, Teddy, and you be nice. Understand?"

"Yeah, I understand. Let's get this over with."

Fred motioned the couple to chairs facing him and Gail, but with their backs to Allison. Allison couldn't figure out exactly why he was allowing her, even encouraging her, to listen to the statements, but she took full advantage of the opportunity.

Again Fred gave his preliminary speech about this not being an official inquiry yet and asked for a brief recounting of events. "We turned in early last night," Teddy began.

"What time was that?" Gail asked. "It's helpful to have the details."

"I'm on vacation," Teddy said. "I don't wear my watch on vacation."

Fred nodded. "Of course. We just want an approximate time."

It was Imogene who supplied the time. "It was close to nine. After dinner I took a walk around the grounds while Teddy talked to Jake. When it started getting dark, I went up to our room to watch TV. We always bring a portable when we come here. I can't go to sleep without TV. An old Errol Flynn movie was on and Teddy came in when it was about over, so it was close to nine o'clock."

"That's right," Teddy agreed.

"So you went to bed at nine?" Again Gail seemed determined to get the exact time.

"Well, we got in bed, but we didn't go to sleep," Imogene said and gave Teddy a sly look. He looked the other way. "That is," she hastened to explain, "we watched TV for another hour or so."

"You didn't leave the room again?" Fred asked.

"No," Teddy said, his voice getting edgy. "We didn't leave the room after nine."

"Oh," Imogene gasped, then put her hand to her mouth as if she would like to recall that last utterance.

Fred, Gail and Teddy all looked at her. Fred spoke. "Was there something else you wanted to tell us?"

"Well, it isn't important. It's just that Teddy did leave for a little bit." She looked at her husband and shrugged her shoulders. "Don't you remember, Honey? You said you were hungry and were going down to the kitchen."

"Yeah. Imogene reminded me there was some banana pudding left. That made me hungry and I went down and finished it."

"All right. And this morning?" Allison thought Fred sounded as if he was getting impatient. Maybe this was taking longer than he'd expected. Or maybe he was beginning to wonder if all this was a waste of time. The medical examiner may say that Bess Lattimer died of natural causes.

"We were up and dressed when Serena knocked on the door and told us the news," Teddy said. "And you know the rest." He stood up, reached for Imogene's hand, and pulled her to her feet. "I've got some business in town to attend to. Okay?"

Fred waved them out. Allison watched them leave the room and hurry toward the back door. She wondered what business dealing he could have here. He lived in Charlotte; his building-supply business operated there. She doubted he would be selling materials this far away. Serena came in. "They're here for Mrs. L."

"Fine," Fred said. "Gail, show them the way and check with the medical examiner if it's all right to move the body."

"Then can I tell my story?" Serena asked. "I have to get to class."

Fred nodded. While waiting for Gail to return, he hunted up the coffee and refilled his cup. Allison remained still. Serena came in, flopped in the chair next to Fred and gave a sigh. "So, what do you want to know?"

Fred put on a fatherly smile. "When do you have time for class? I know you work here in the mornings and then at Cassie's Seafood in the afternoons."

"Oh, I squeeze in a couple of classes at Clement Tech before lunch. Going to be a nurse." Allison noticed she sat up a little straighter as she made that announcement. "I've been taking the basics so far, anatomy and pharmacology this summer. Then in the fall I'll start the nursing classes. Mrs. L. told me she was going to be leaving, so I didn't feel bad about quitting my job here."

Gail came back into the room and picked up her notebook. "Mrs. Lattimer told you she was leaving?"

"Yeah. But I didn't think she meant this way."

Gail's pen was ready. "What time did you arrive this morning?"

"Seven, like I always do. I fixed her oatmeal. She alternated between oatmeal and bran flakes. This was an oatmeal day." Allison watched fascinated as Gail scribbled away, and wondered if a tape recorder wouldn't be more efficient. Serena repeated the same story she had told Allison and Paul earlier, almost as if she had rehearsed it, Allison thought.

"What did you do after you had awakened the others?" Fred asked.

"Went back in and straightened up the room. Picked up the medicine bottles scattered on the floor."

"Why?" Allison sensed the annoyance in Fred's question.

"Because that's part of my job—fixing up the room, that is. After Mrs. L. eats breakfast, she gets up, goes to her recliner by the window and reads while I make up the bed and straighten up the room. I figured I ought to do it this morning too, even though she wasn't going to get out of bed."

"Was the bed messed up much? Any more than usual?" Gail's eyes left her notebook long enough to ask.

"Not particularly, though one of her pillows was on the floor. Mrs. L. always slept on two pillows, to help her breathe better, you know. But one pillow was beside the bed, along with the medicine bottles."

"What did you make of this?" Fred asked.

"I just figured she had a bad spell and knocked

things over trying to get to her inhaler. She does have spells, you know, when she can't get her breath." Serena checked her watch. "My class starts in a few minutes. Can I go now?"

Fred nodded. Gail looked at her notebook and shook her head. "Not much detail about which bottles were on the floor or where they landed. I hope she can do better when we question her again."

"So you think we'll be coming back?"

"Sure do."

"In that case, let's speed up the preliminary questions. We can go deeper later, if we have to, after the autopsy report."

Fred motioned to Allison. "Would you mind asking Charles to come in now?"

"And the children?"

"No. Let them play. We don't need to talk to them, at least, not now."

Charles started out with his usual studied smile, but his handsome face sagged in weariness. Allison hadn't talked to Charles much. She only knew that he was an ardent environmentalist. Catherine had hinted that his crusades to save the planet had destroyed his marriage. Right now he didn't look much like a crusader. His shoulders slumped, and his eyes darted nervously between the two officers. His voice was soft and measured. "What can I do for you?"

"Just tell me a little about last night and this morning," Fred instructed.

"There's not much to tell. It'd been a busy day for the kids. They were tired and ready for bed early. I tucked them in and then went to bed myself. I was up and dressed and checking on Becky when I saw Serena come up the stairs with Aunt Bess's tray. Then in a few minutes she was knocking on my door with the news."

Gail asked her usual question, "And what time last night did you go to your room?"

"I'm not sure. Probably about nine. Teddy was right ahead of us. Becky ran and gave him a good-night kiss."

"Did you watch TV?" Fred asked.

Charles looked surprised. "No. There aren't any TVs in the bedrooms—except Teddy's. He brings his own. I didn't feel like going downstairs to watch."

"So you went right to bed?"

"I read a magazine for a few minutes, got sleepy, and went to bed."

Allison squirmed. Something wasn't quite right, she thought, but whatever was teasing her mind slid out as Fred continued. "Seems like everyone went to bed early. No late night family reminiscing? I under-stand you hadn't seen your cousins in quite a while. You didn't want to talk to them? Catch up on the latest news?"

Charles shrugged. "Not last night. We'd all gotten up early, spent hours on the road, and then Aunt Bess horrified us with her news. I guess we were too tired and too numb to talk much."

Fred put his coffee cup down slowly and sat up straighter. "And what was your aunt's news?"

With some hesitation Charles repeated what had

gone on in the family meeting. His version was much like what Allison had heard from Catherine, although he left out much of how he and the others had reacted. "It almost seemed to me," Charles went on, "that Aunt Bess had considered all the possibilities for the Blue Goose and had chosen the one that would hurt us the most."

Fred gazed thoughtfully at the solemn young man in front of him. "Why would she do that?"

"I don't know. I thought about it all last evening. Maybe she'd decided we hadn't shown proper appreciation for all she'd done for us."

"Had you?"

"No," Charles said. "She wasn't an easy person to like, to appreciate. I guess that's not much of an excuse, but it's the truth."

"You were upset about your aunt's decision to clear-cut the land?"

"Of course. We all were. It would have ruined the entire area."

"And now that won't happen? Her death changes the future of the Blue Goose?"

"I guess so. She was going to sign the papers this morning. But since she didn't…"

Fred nodded. "Since she didn't, the lodge and acreage are saved. Do you know what is in her will?"

Charles took a deep breath, his eyes came alive, and a hint of a smile played on his lips. "As far as I know, the estate goes equally to the four of us."

Fred glanced at Gail, and she nodded her head. Allison was sure they were thinking the same thing.

Motives! Allison was smug with the thought, however, that the motive issue would not apply to her friend. Cat had just wanted to sell the place and give money for medical research, surely an unselfish desire. Her smugness was shaken when Charles added, "One thing Aunt Bess said to Catherine, though, didn't make sense to me. She told her, 'The money will go to treat my disease, not yours.' You might want to ask Catherine about it."

"Yes I'll do that. You can go now, and please ask Catherine to come in."

Fred appeared impatient when Catherine didn't show up immediately. Jake could be seen sitting at the dining room table with Lillian hovering over him, urging him to eat something. Fred motioned them both to come into the library. Jake's eyes were flame red, and he still clutched his matted handkerchief. Lillian had composed herself and asked if the detectives wanted more coffee or perhaps a cinnamon roll or doughnut. They declined. Allison was beginning to feel the effects of no breakfast. She would have gladly given a pint of blood for a chocolate eclair, but Lillian didn't extend the offer her way, and she was fearful of missing something if she left her post.

Fred addressed himself to Jake first. The garrulous old man of last evening was gone and in his place was a taciturn witness determined not to say more than he had to. "Ate dinner. Bess tired. She went to bed. I talked to Teddy. Went home."

"How did you come and go?" Gail asked, "and at what times?"

"Boat. Rowed over. Don't drive anymore, too far to walk. Came six. Left eight."

"Good," Fred said. "And you, Lillian?"

"I cleaned up after dinner like I always do. Nobody ate much, though, except Teddy. I didn't understand that. I served country ham with sweet-potato casserole, three-bean salad, English peas and made-from-scratch biscuits. Now I ask you, who could want a better meal?"

Fred grinned. "Sounds good to me. Any left-overs?"

"Plenty. Want some?" Lillian's gracious smile spoke of a woman who loved to share the bounty of her kitchen.

"No, but thanks anyway," Fred said. "Actually we might have to take them to be examined."

The smile vanished. "Are you thinking it was my cooking that killed poor Bess? I'll have you know I've been cooking here for more than thirty years and never had the first complaint."

Allison covered her mouth to stifle a giggle. It looks like Fred just lost a friend, she thought. It's not likely Lillian will ever offer him any more food.

Fred shrugged his shoulders and went on, "Then what did you do after you cleaned up?"

"I started the dishwasher, fed some scraps to Lancelot and went home."

Catherine entered the library, gave a surprised glance at Allison and then focused on the detectives. Fred tried to dismiss Lillian and Jake, "Thanks, that'll be all for now."

But Lillian had something else on her mind. "Bess promised me a good amount in severance pay. You know she was planning on moving out West?"

"Yes, so I've been told."

"The trouble is I don't know what will happen now. You reckon the cousins will give me anything? It'd be hard to find another job at my age."

"I'm sure they'll be fair," Fred said. "You just need to talk to them about it." He smiled and motioned her to the door.

Lillian relinquished her seat and Catherine sat down. "So I guess you went to bed with the birds like everybody else?" Fred asked.

Catherine gave him a puzzled look. "Actually, no. Allison and I went for a ride around the lake with Paul. The house was dark when we came in. I guess it was about ten or ten-thirty." She looked back at her friend. "Is that right, Allison?"

"I think so. I didn't see a clock." Allison could feel Gail's disappointment. The young detective was so determined to get accurate times down in her notebook.

Now it was Fred's turn to look puzzled. "Paul? Who's he? Why haven't I heard about him?"

"A friend, or rather a neighbor. That is, he has a camper on the property next to this one." Catherine seemed at a loss to further explain Paul and then added, "He's here on vacation."

"But where is he now? I might want to talk to him."

"Fishing. We were down at the dock, and when I came up he said he was going fishing. He's on vacation, you know."

"I know. You just told me." Fred sighed. "That's all right. I can catch him later. But there's one thing you can clear up for me now, Catherine."

"Yes?"

"What did your aunt mean when she stated the money was not going to *your* disease?"

Allison carefully watched her friend's face. There wasn't a flicker of surprise or worry. "It's just that I wanted her to give some money for cancer research and she wasn't interested in donating anything. That's all."

She's lying, Allison thought. Cat had expected the question and had her answer ready. But why lie about it? And what was the real answer?

Their questioning done for now, Fred instructed Gail to be sure Bess's medications were bagged, then asked Catherine to give him a tour of the premises. As they left the room, Fred turned to Allison, "Thanks for your help."

Allison felt a blush creeping up and nodded her head as she turned away. Gail started out of the room and then turned abruptly, came back to Allison, and whispered, "Fred's taken a shine to you, gal."

"Shine? What are you talking about?"

"He likes you." Gail gave her a big grin. "I've been working with him for a year, and I can read that old bachelor like a book."

After Gail left, Allison tried to remember her exact words, but she was only sure of two of them: "shine" and "bachelor." They were enough to put a smile on her face for the rest of the morning.

SEVEN

It was late afternoon when Fred Sawyer called from his office and asked to speak to Charles. Since Charles was the eldest of the cousins, Fred had arbitrarily appointed him head of the Blue Goose gang. And as such, Charles's first task would be to inform the others of the medical examiner's preliminary report. "There were traces of cyanide found in the body," Fred said. "That means we'll have to investigate the death as a possible homicide."

Silence congealed on the phone line between the lake and the sheriff's office. Then Fred heard a gasp and Charles's unbelieving voice. "Cyanide? This can't be happening. It must be a mistake or an accident."

"Could be," Fred said, although he knew it couldn't be. He didn't want to argue the case yet. "We'll get it all sorted out in a few days. In the meantime, our deputies have a search warrant to go over the entire lodge, including each of your rooms."

"What am I to tell Teddy and the others?"

"Exactly what I've told you," Fred said. "Deputies Sam Patterson and Dominic Matrillo will be there shortly."

"They're already here," Charles interrupted, "if you're talking about two big fellows in uniform. You people don't waste any time, do you?"

"Not if we can help it," Fred replied calmly. "As I started to say, Sam and Dominic will be looking around and asking a few questions. I believe we'll leave the fingerprinting until later."

"Fingerprints?" Charles shouted.

Fred ignored the outburst. "Let me talk to one of the deputies." He waited patiently while the phone clicked and footsteps shuffled.

"Sam here." He listened as Fred gave him further instructions. "We'll take care of everything for now, Sir."

When Fred hung up, Gail commented, "You certainly didn't tell the family much."

"Didn't intend to. All that bunch needs to know now is that we're going to be investigating."

"Well, at least we can narrow down the time of death from the autopsy," Gail said, consulting her notebook. "The report put it between eight and ten. But since Derita spoke to Bess at nine-thirty, that only leaves a half-hour window."

"So it seems," Fred commented. "Frankly, I'm more concerned about how the cyanide was administered." Fred massaged his chin, rubbed his nose and wiped his eyes. In the past, these procedures had been known to stimulate his brain cells. But not this time. He picked up the report again, "Traces of cyanide. So how did it get there? In her food or pills? Skin absorption? Inhalation? This isn't going to be easy. Maybe further lab tests will tell us something."

ALLISON HAD SEEN the police car drive up and had opened the door for the deputies. When she heard Charles repeat the words, "cyanide" and "fingerprints" she knew it had to be a detective on the other end of the line. Curiosity swept over her like a tidal wave.

She saw Charles hand over the phone to the deputy, and then collapse in the nearest chair. His usual self-assured demeanor had evaporated under the news. Sam hung up the phone and turned to Charles. "Mr. Sawyer says the family can go ahead with the funeral arrangements. The medical examiner will probably release the body tomorrow. You're to let us know where and when the funeral will be. He'll get back with you after that."

Charles nodded. Allison waited for the deputy to make a further explanation of the medical examiner findings. He didn't.

She introduced herself to the deputies, told them the rest of the family had taken yard chairs down to the lake and were watching the children swim. "They thought it would take their minds off this terrible business for a little bit. Want me to call them up?"

"Not yet," Sam said. "We'll talk to them later." Allison had to tilt her head back a little to talk to him. He was at least six-four, built like a wrestler, and had a face guaranteed to scare babies. I'd hate to get on his wrong side, she thought.

Dominic, on the other hand, gave her a smile as big as a Moon Pie. "Would you be so kind to show us to Mrs. Lattimer's room?"

THE FUNERAL WAS HELD the next day at Knott's Funeral Home. Allison scanned the small group of mourners. Derita's parents had flown in for the service. Allison had met them only briefly. They had chosen to stay at a motel rather than at the lodge. Lawrence Lattimer was Henry's brother. He'd said he had little contact with his sister-in-law since Henry's death, but family was family. And for Derita's sake, he felt they needed to attend the funeral, no matter how much time had elapsed since their last visit.

Charles's ex-wife, Vera June, had arrived early that morning. She'd driven down to be there for the children. She was sitting between them now, an arm around each of them. She had dark blond hair, the color of wet sand, which looked like it had just been towel-dried in a hurry. Allison wondered if it had been her natural look which had attracted Charles, the nature lover, in the first place. Charles was next to Wesley with his arm across the back of the seat, his fingers touching the back of Vera June's neck. They could have been the picture of a perfect family, Allison mused.

But she knew from personal experience that families were often not what they appeared to be. Marriages were more fragile than life itself and could be killed by poisons much less lethal than cyanide.

Vera June had announced her intention of taking the children home right after the funeral. "We'll go back to the lodge for lunch and get their things and then head for home," she'd said. Charles had agreed it would be for the best.

Allison's gaze shifted to Teddy and Imogene sitting in the front row. Imogene had made a trip to town the day before to buy a black dress: long sleeves, high cut neckline, mid-calf skirt. Allison saw Catherine nudge Derita and heard her whisper, "She reminds me of the evil Madame X we used to watch on Saturday mornings' TV. Hasn't anybody told her that funeral black isn't mandatory anymore?"

"Remember she's an actress," Derita whispered back. "To her this is a stage and she's playing the part to the hilt." Allison got tickled when Derita's mother leaned over and shushed her daughter. Derita gave her mother an embarrassed nod and sat meekly back in her seat.

Lillian, Serena, and Jake had taken seats in the back and were joined by a handful of others, who, Allison presumed, were local acquaintances. Gail slid in beside them just before the service started.

Allison wished Paul had come. He had suggested that to Catherine this morning, but she'd shaken her head. "No. You'll feel out of place and besides you didn't even know her."

"True," he said. "But I know you and I can be there if you need me."

Allison wanted to shake her friend when she'd answered, "Thanks, but I'll be fine." Allison couldn't understand why Catherine seemed determined to push away any man who tried to get close.

The service was short and unsentimental. Probably what Bess would have wanted, Allison thought, from what little she knew of the woman. The minister of the church spoke of Bess Lattimer's good deeds and generous purse. "Although her health prevented her from often attending our church, she never failed in her financial support. She will be sorely missed by her church, her community and her family."

Allison didn't listen to much of the sermon. Her thoughts were on the unfinished business of solving the terrible crime which had been committed. One of the people in this room is a murderer. It was hard for her to fathom the fact. Allison had never intentionally hurt anyone in her life. How could she get inside the mind of a person who not only was willing to hurt—but to kill? She had to do it, though. Mr. Sawyer had said he needed all the help he could get, and she believed him. She felt he was a fine man and probably a good detective, but surely murder was not an everyday occurrence in this little county. She doubted that he'd had much experience along that line. Not that I have, she admitted to herself, but it can't be much harder than solving the brain teasers in the Reader's Digest. Allison didn't know when the detectives would be back out to the Blue Goose to continue their investigation, but she decided to start the minute everyone got back to the lodge.

The dining room table was loaded with offerings by neighbors and town folks: casseroles, salads, cobblers, and KFC. Bess Lattimer had not encouraged visitors to the lodge during the past several years, but today the curious and the kindhearted came, bearing sustenance and sympathy. The funeral goers changed from church clothes back into casual wear before heading for the table. Allison and Catherine slid back into comfortable jeans while Derita opted for white deck pants. Imogene, on the other hand, appeared reluctant to give up her mourning garb. She now appeared in black stretch pants and a long-sleeved black shirt.

Allison wanted to spend some time with Catherine discussing what the cousins had started calling "the situation." Teddy had announced he had to get back to Charlotte as soon as the situation was settled. Charles told Vera June and the children he would stop by and see them as soon as he could, but he didn't know how long it would take to clear up the situation. Derita's parents, who were flying back home in the morning, told her not to worry about this sordid situation—that the police would have it cleared up in a few days. They assured her it must be an accident or that the coroner had simply made a mistake. Allison was amazed that none of them really seemed to accept the fact that Bess had been murdered.

But Allison did believe it, and she knew one of them was hiding a terrible secret. When she approached Catherine, though, her friend didn't want to talk about it. "It's too awful. I can't face it right now." Catherine looked around at the family members, each with a Styrofoam plate and a plastic fork. "And I can't face any of them now, either." She took a plate, piled it high with a little of everything, grabbed two forks and headed out the door. "I'm going to find Paul."

Allison was momentarily angry at being dumped, but was glad Catherine had not completely turned her back on Paul. She quickly decided this was her opportunity to speak to the others, but she didn't know quite where to begin. Charles and Vera June seemed to be having a serious conversation in the porch swing, Wesley was idly kicking the soccer ball and Becky was wandering around by the garage. Teddy was talking to Jake, Imogene announced she was going to lie down for a few minutes, and Derita had gone back upstairs after her parents left. Serena had headed out the back door saying she had to get home and do some studying. That left Lillian. Allison found her in the kitchen, not busy as Allison had expected, but sitting on a stool in the corner, staring at the sink.

Allison went up and touched the housekeeper's shoulder. "You're going to miss her, aren't you?"

Lillian nodded and swiped at some tears. "It's not that we were friends. We were never that. She was boss and I was hired help. But we were used to each other. She wasn't easy to please, believe me." Lillian almost smiled, wiping away another escaping tear. "She felt it was her bounded duty to find fault with at least one thing every day. She said she didn't want me to get uppity. But I knew she liked me and the way I did things. She just couldn't bring herself to say it. Can you understand that?"

"Yes, I think I can understand. Some people have trouble showing love, or even tenderness."

"But she paid me good. Even when times were getting hard, she'd often add a little extra to my check. She never said anything about it. And she didn't want me to say anything either or thank her for it. Like I said, we understood each other."

"But her nieces and nephews didn't—understand her, that is?"

"Derita was the only one who even tried. The others just gave her back what they thought she gave them—sharp words and hard feelings."

Allison nodded her head. "I see." She reached over the counter and pulled a box of tissues closer as Lillian's eyes again overflowed. She felt sorry for the aging housekeeper, but decided it was time to get on with the business at hand. "Lillian, if it's not too much for you, could you tell me a little more of what happened that evening? It might help clarify some things for me. Did you notice what the others were doing?"

"Like I told that detective, no one ate much, except Teddy. Teddy always did appreciate my cooking. When everybody left the table, I was busy clearing up. Everybody just kind of scattered. I know Bess went up to her room early, but I think she and Jake talked a little before she went up. Charles and Teddy wanted to start a game of horseshoes with the children. I heard Wesley and Becky arguing that they each wanted to be partners with their Uncle Teddy because he was a better player than their father. Then when Jake came out of the house, Teddy said he didn't feel like playing and went over to talk to Jake. They were standing on the porch and I could see them through the open door. Teddy must have asked Jake something because I saw Jake shake his head and then Teddy raised both his fists in the air like he wanted to hit something or somebody."

"Was Imogene with him?"

"No. Come to think of it, I didn't see Imogene. She was probably somewhere looking in a mirror. When that hussy isn't hanging onto Teddy's arm, she's either taking a nap or looking in a mirror.

"I did see Derita though. She helped Bess to her room in the elevator. She's been doing that every night since she's been here—what with the night nurse being gone and all. She's been real sweet to Bess, even more than usual.

"And of course, I saw you and Catherine take off for a boat ride with that new fellow around here. That's all I know. I finished cleaning up and went home, which is what I'm going to do right now."

Allison thanked Lillian for her help, although she doubted if any of the information would be helpful to the investigation. She wanted to talk to Jake again, but when she came out on the porch, she saw the old man heading for his rowboat to go home. Allison was wondering what direction to head next when she heard Charles and Vera June calling for Becky.

"Where in the world could that child have gotten to?" Vera June started circling the house. "Becky, you get your tail up here. We've got to leave now to get home before dark."

"Wesley, you look down by the lake," Charles said. "I'll check out the back yard."

Allison sensed trouble and, as usual, wanted to help. She came up to Charles. "What seems to be the matter?"

"Vera June's ready to leave and we can't find Becky. It's not like her to wander off. Could you check the house? She might be reading somewhere. When she gets her nose in a book she wouldn't know if the roof fell in."

Allison searched the house. Derita heard the commotion and joined Vera June. Teddy was practicing some golf swings when he heard the shouting and was soon tramping through bushes, looking under overgrown hedges, and calling for his niece. Allison saw Wesley heading for Catherine and Paul who were sitting on the pier. The three of them started scouring the lakeside. Paul turned over a row boat that had been resting upside down since last summer. Two startled toads blinked in the bright sunlight and hopped to the safety of some nearby weeds.

The voices, which at first had shown annoyance and impatience, began to sound increasingly alarmed as minutes passed with no sign of the missing girl.

Imogene came out onto the porch rubbing her eyes. "What's all the racket about? I was trying to take a nap."

Vera June came up the steps, tears staining her cheeks. "Becky's gone. We can't find her anywhere."

"Becky? Oh, my God!" Imogene crossed the porch in two steps and enveloped Vera June in her arms. "How terrible. Dear, sweet Becky."

Vera June sobbed into Imogene's embrace. "Oh, where's my baby? Where is she?"

Catherine and Paul clambered up the hill. Catherine came up to Charles. "Shouldn't we call the police? Get a search party? Good heavens, we've got to do something!"

Charles shook his head in bewilderment. "I just don't understand it. What could have happened to my little girl?" His voice broke and he crumbled on the porch steps.

Paul sat down beside him and put an arm around the heaving shoulders. "Do you want me to pray?"

Charles lifted his head and stared at the other man, a man whom he had met only days earlier and had spoken to only a few times. "Please," he cried. It was only a single word, but it was a plea from an anguished heart.

Tears stung at Catherine's eyes. "We need something more than a little prayer!" She ran in the house and called the sheriff's department.

EIGHT

FRED HADN'T PLANNED TO RETURN to the Lattimer house until the next day, and when the call came in about a missing child, he sent two deputies out to assist in the search. Gail asked him if she could accompany them. He agreed. Then he spent several minutes arguing with himself out loud. "Can't be any connection to the murder. The girl just wandered off in the woods and they'll find her, probably scared, but unharmed." His gentle, reasonable brain kept telling him, *No one would want to hurt a child.* But the other side of his brain, the reality-hardened part that had seen human depravity, that had stared into the face of horror one too many times, convinced him otherwise. His own car was soon on the narrow twisted road leading to Lake Lucia.

WHILE THEY WERE WAITING for the sheriff's deputies to arrive, Allison watched in admiration as Teddy took charge of the search. "Now, we can't panic. Let's get organized. Catherine, you and Paul go back to the lake. Check the boathouse, scour every inch of the shore. Charles and Derita can head toward the cemetery. That's just the kind of place a kid might explore. She might not have realized how far it is or how overgrown the path." He attempted a smile. "Remember how we used to sneak over there, Charles?" Charles nodded and Allison thought she saw a flicker of hope in his eyes. Teddy went on, "Imogene and I will start in the woods.

"Allison, you stay here with Vera June and Wesley. When the cops get here, send them out the cemetery way. I still think that's our best bet." No wonder he does well in business, Allison thought. He certainly knows how to give orders. It was only when everyone had scattered that Allison wondered why Teddy had commandeered the woods for himself. Could it be he was more concerned about the little yellow flags not being found than about finding Becky? She reminded herself, the first chance she got, she would tell Fred about the work that had gone on in the woods. She had begun to call the detective by his first name in her mind, and already considered him a friend. But she couldn't dwell on that. Finding Becky was the most important thing now.

Allison tried to get Vera June to stop her pacing and sit on one of the porch chairs. She called Wesley to her. "How about going to the kitchen and finding your mother something cold to drink?"

"Yes'um." Allison's heart broke for the little boy who was trying not to let his fear show. He came back with Diet Cokes for the women and an orange drink for himself. As he handed Allison her drink, he asked, "Reckon they'll find Becky soon?"

"I'm sure they will. There's the police car now. You stay with your mother while I talk to them." Allison saw Sam, Dominic and Gail get out of the car. Allison was disappointed not to see Fred also, but didn't ask about him. She filled the deputies in on what had happened and where everyone was searching.

"You say she's twelve," Sam repeated. "My little girl will be twelve next month. It'd kill me if anything happened to her." His stone face softened and Allison thought she glimpsed a touch of moisture in his eyes.

Vera June came running up as Sam was speaking. "Then you know how I feel," she cried. "Please, please, you've got to find Becky."

"We will, Ma'am," Sam assured her. "If we don't come up with anything in the next little bit, we'll send for more men and a helicopter and maybe a boat."

"A boat?" Vera June swayed a little and Allison put an arm around her. "Surely you don't think she's in the water?"

"We have a boat," Allison said. "That is, a neighbor has a pontoon. Do you think he ought to use that?"

"It might be a good idea," Gail said, as the men headed into the brush toward the cemetery.

Allison started down the hill. "I'll tell him."

Gail called after her, "Has anyone checked in back of the lodge and the garage?"

"I think one of the men did, but I'm not sure."

When Allison reached the pier, she saw Catherine and Paul coming out of the boathouse. Catherine was shaking as if gripped in a chill, although the temperature was in the eighties. "No one has been in there for years," Paul said, brushing cobwebs out of his hair and beard. Allison told him what Gail had suggested. "Good idea. I'll bring it around to the dock and you can get on, Catherine."

Catherine looked terrible. It's like she already knows what we're going to find, Allison thought, and it's going to be hellish. "I think Catherine better come up to the house with me." Allison reached out and took her friend's hand. "She can keep Vera June and Wesley company."

"No!" Catherine pulled away from Allison's touch. "I'm going with Paul. We've got to find her— no matter what—no matter where."

Allison retraced her steps to the house. She would check on Vera June and then start searching also. She didn't know which direction to take, but she had to do something. As she came up on the porch, she heard another car. Was it just relief she felt when she saw Fred get out, or was it a bit of pleasure too? He certainly wasn't handsome with his paunchy belly and thinning hair, but he exuded an air of confidence combined with gentleness which Allison admired. She blushed remembering how kindly he had treated her. She hurried up to him. "I'm so glad you're here." Then realizing how that might sound, she quickly added, "We need all the help we can get."

"Let's think a little bit," Fred said, "before we

start off on a wild goose chase. Just suppose there's a connection between Becky's disappearance and the murder. What could possibly make that connection?"

Allison hadn't thought of it before, but now that she did, the idea didn't seem too far-fetched. "Becky may have found something. Or heard something. And the murderer had to keep her quiet."

"Right. They would have to stop her from talking and then hide her…" Fred stopped in mid-sentence, and looked up at the sky.

Allison caught her breath. "You were going to say, 'hide her body,' weren't you?"

Fred shook his head. "Let's not go there. Just think of possible hiding places."

"But there's acres and acres where she could be hidden. We'll have to cover every inch."

"I don't think so. There wasn't time to go far. And even though Becky is only twelve, she still isn't exactly tiny. I remember seeing her and I'd say she weighs at least eighty pounds. Even a strong man like me couldn't have carried her a long distance in a short time."

Allison studied the man in front of her and decided she wouldn't mind being carried away by a man like that. Then ashamed of herself, she brought her mind back to Becky. "She could have been lured away. Someone could have said, 'Come here, Becky. I've got something to show you.'"

Fred jumped in, "And since she knew the person and wasn't afraid, she followed him, or her, until they were out of sight of the others and then—whatever happened, happened."

Allison shivered. She didn't want to think about what might have happened. Gail appeared from what had once been part of the lodge's parking lot, but was now grown up with shrubs and weeds. "Nothing out there that I can see." Gail approached them with a piece of paper in her hand. "But I did find this in the garage. Don't know if it means anything. Looks like part of a label from a medicine bottle."

Fred reached for the paper and read out loud, ".06%. Federal law prohibits…" He showed the bit of paper to Allison. She could clearly see where it had been torn.

"It's a prescription label," Gail said. "Not over the counter. Why would it be in the garage?"

"I don't know. But we're going find out." Fred ran the few feet to the garage door with Allison and Gail right behind him.

The garage appeared as Allison remembered it when she and Catherine had gotten out the lawnmower. Instead of cars, the garage housed an assortment of yard chairs, lawn equipment, bug sprays, fertilizer, hoses, old paint cans, cardboard boxes. "Looks like it's just used for storage," Gail said. "I didn't see anything out of the ordinary except that label."

"Where did you find it?" Fred asked.

"Right there by the door where we came in. I didn't notice it until I was leaving, then I almost stepped on it."

Fred bent down and examined the area. "Could have been there for months."

Allison shook her head. "I don't think so. Catherine and I came in to get the lawnmower the other day. If it'd been laying there, one of us would probably have stepped on it and left some dirt or grass stain." She pointed at the slip of paper in Fred's hand. "It's perfectly clean, not even a smudge."

"You're right," Fred agreed. "We'll check Mrs. Lattimer's medicine bottles when we get back to the office, see if any of them have a torn label."

"It's a liquid," Allison said.

Gail jerked her head and looked at Allison. "How do you know that?"

"The percentage. You read '.06 %'. Pills aren't labeled in percentages. It has to be a liquid or a spray or an inhaler."

Gail patted Allison on the back. "Like Fred likes to say, 'We can use all the help we can get.'"

Allison was relieved to hear Gail's remark. Earlier she had felt Gail might resent her presence, but now she felt like one of the team.

Fred started to leave. "I'll call in and have someone check out those medication bottles."

"Wait a minute." Allison stared at the ancient lawnmower they had used on the jungle of a yard. "That's not where Cat parked the mower when we finished with it. She pushed it back in the other corner where we'd found it." The mower was now leaning against some cardboard boxes as if to keep them in place. Fred took two giant strides, jerked the lawnmower handle away, and the boxes came tumbling down.

ALLISON SCREAMED, Gail covered her mouth, and Fred bent over the battered girl.

He tried not to think of the pretty girl he had noticed a few days earlier running across the front yard, playing kickball with her brother. He pushed back her matted dark hair and felt for a carotid pulse. It was faint, but it was there. "She's alive. Call an ambulance." Gail fled to the house. Fred's impulse was to cradle the child in his arms, to whisper hope to the unconscious brain, to let her know that love was still here. Instead, he slid back so as not to disturb the scene or move the girl in any way. Allison tried to get close, but he shoved her back. "Tell the family we've found her and that she's alive. But don't let any of them in here."

ALLISON RAN TO DO as she was told. On the way she stopped at Catherine's car and gave several loud blasts on the horn. She didn't know if there was a correct signal, but she figured the searchers would hear it and come in to see what it was about. Allison met Vera June bolting from the porch. Gail came up at the same time and it took both of them to keep the distraught mother from running to her daughter. "The ambulance will be here soon," Gail said. "You can follow it to the hospital. Becky's unconscious and we don't want to do anything that might harm her further. Detective Sawyer is staying with her."

"What happened to my baby?" Vera June sobbed. "What happened?"

"We don't know. She may have fallen and hit her

head." Gail turned Vera June around and led her to a chair. "But we don't want anyone to disturb the area until we know for sure."

Allison put her arms around Wesley who was huddled on the porch steps. "We think Becky will be all right, but she has to go to the hospital. You stay here with your mother. Your daddy and the others should be here soon."

"Okay." Wesley sniffed, went over to where his mother was sitting, slid down to the floor and put his head in her lap.

Paul didn't bother docking the pontoon. He threw out the anchor, then he and Catherine jumped into the water and waded to shore. Allison flew down the hill as they scrambled up. "We found Becky," she shouted on her way down. "She got hit on the head and she's unconscious, but she's alive!"

"Thank God," Catherine cried, squeezing Allison's hands. "Thank God."

Paul bowed his head. "Yes, Lord. We thank you."

As the ambulance prepared to leave the parking area, Allison saw Fred motion to Vera June. "You can ride with Becky, but no one else." Charles ran up and tried to get into the ambulance, but Fred kept him back. "You'd better stay with the boy." Charles didn't argue. He grabbed Wesley's arm, piled him into the car, and raced out of the drive right behind the ambulance.

Teddy and Imogene bolted to their car. Imogene called to Derita, "You can ride with us."

Derita shook her head, "I'll drive by myself."

Catherine hesitated, looked down at her wet jeans. Paul came over to her. "Go ahead, I'll see that you get some dry clothes. I know you want to be there." Catherine gave him a grateful smile, sprang into her car and followed the caravan.

Fred told Sam to follow all of them. "Stay out of the way, but keep your eyes open." He turned to Dominic. "Call the emergency room and tell them we suspect attempted murder."

Dominic's Latin eyes opened wide in surprise. "We do?"

"Yes, we do. Gail will fill you in. You two go over the garage again: fingerprints, possible weapons, the whole bit."

Paul stood looking after the cars and then turned to Allison. "I need to take Catherine some dry clothes. Could you get some from her room?" Allison motioned him to follow her. She gathered a change of clothing and found a plastic bag. "Good," said Paul. "I'll scoot on home, change into something dry myself and then drive to the hospital. Want to go with me?"

"No. I'm going to stay here, but call me with any news about Becky." Paul started for the stairs. "And Paul," Allison called out, "thanks for being a friend to Cat."

As she started down the hallway, Allison noticed the door to Bess Lattimer's bedroom was open. Her curiosity pulled her down the hall. She peered over the yellow crime scene tape and saw Fred surveying the room. He'd removed his jacket, rolled up his shirt sleeves, loosened his tie, and was looking baffled. Allison cleared her throat and got the detective's attention. "Could I possibly come in, Mr. Sawyer?"

He smiled and waved her in. "The room's been gone over, dusted and all, so we can't do any damage. And it's 'Fred' if you want to try to help with this puzzle, Mrs. Aldridge."

"I'll help in any way I can. And please call me 'Allison.'"

"Well, Allison," Fred pointed to a box of medications on top of the dresser. "The meds which Bess was currently using were bagged and sent in, but Serena called me later and said that the prescriptions had been recently refilled. These new bottles were in the bottom drawer."

"Anything with a torn label?"

"No. And no label with the dosage written as a percentage. But I just called our office. One of the bottles we confiscated did have such a label. It's a nasal spray, but the label was complete. So we're back to the question of where is the bottle which belongs to our scrap of label?"

"And what was it doing in the garage?" Allison added.

Fred rubbed his chin that was getting a little dark around the edges. "Do you know if trash from the house is placed in the garage?"

"I don't think so. I saw Lillian empty some trash in the can outside the kitchen door. She told me Jake comes by once a week and carries the can to the end of the driveway for the county truck to empty. Come to think of it, I remember seeing the can at the drive the day we arrived."

"So if they come once a week that means everything placed in the can since that day is still there."

Allison frowned. "You mean we should search the trash can?"

"Not we. But I'm sure Gail and Dominic would be delighted to do it. I'll suggest it when we go down."

Allison looked around the room. "So-o-o, what's next?"

"We'll have all the meds, both these and the others, analyzed. I doubt, though, if the murderer left any poison for us to find."

"Fred," Allison said hesitantly, "I don't mean to be nosy…"

"But you are. So out with it. What do you want to know?"

"Just what did Dr. Caldwell see that made him suspicious in the first place?"

"Pink skin."

"Pink skin? But shouldn't her skin have been pink?"

"Not her back. Not with postmortem lividity. Parts of the deceased body that are in contact with a surface normally change from pink to reddish brown to deep purple depending on the amount of lapsed time. It's due to blood settling to the lowest parts of the body after the heart stops." Allison thought Fred was pleased with the chance to expound his expertise. "Dr. Caldwell knew Bess had been dead over six hours because of the rigor mortis. Yet there were still areas of pinkish coloration on her back." Fred went on, "It could be an indication of some poisonings, including cyanide. Doc picked up on it right away. I was skeptical, though. I thought it might have had something to do with her health problems or her medications. I should have believed him."

"Where would a person get cyanide?"

"Some forms aren't hard to come by. It wouldn't surprise me to find cyanide in the garage right now: old insecticides, poison dusts for plants. Before Henry died, he had a full time gardener who kept these grounds looking like a show place. From what I could see, old supplies were never cleaned out or thrown away. They were just tossed into the garage and left. Any of the suspects could have had access to whatever was there."

"That's another thing, Fred. My head says somebody in the family is the culprit, but my heart has a hard time believing it. Especially now. I can concede that Bess Lattimer was not the most loved person around, but it's hard to imagine how anyone could purposely hurt, much less try to kill, a sweet kid like Becky."

"Self protection. You're the one who suggested Becky may have found or heard something incriminating. I think you're right. She had to be silenced."

"So you think the person who hit and then hid Becky left her for dead?"

"Yes. Then that person went out and joined the search."

"Are you saying that Derita or Teddy or Imogene is the guilty person?"

"Or Charles or Catherine or Paul or Jake or Lillian or you."

"Me?" Allison gasped and stared at Fred, hoping to see a smile. There was none. "You're kidding— right? I've been helping you."

"Many murderers have been helpful in the past, finding clues which point to other people. In fact, many murderers are very nice people." After a few moments Fred gave Allison the smile she wanted. "No, I don't really consider you a suspect. Not that you couldn't have done it, but I can't think of any motive you might have. You don't profit by Bess's death like many of the others. And as far as I've been able to find out, you never knew her before this week. I just wanted to point out the adage that no one is above suspicion."

NINE

FRED'S EYES ROAMED around Bess's room one more time. "If there were any clues here after the murder, they were gone by the time our people got here. Serena, bless her heart, did her best to clean up the crime scene."

Allison liked Serena and rushed to her defense. "You can't blame her. She didn't know it was a crime scene at the time."

"Or so she says."

Allison put her hands on her hips and blocked Fred's exit from the room. "I never met anyone in my life with such a suspicious mind. Are you putting Serena on the suspect list now?"

Fred grinned at Allison's agitation. "Not officially. But I'll do some checking on her whereabouts the night of the murder."

Remembering the yellow flag she had picked up in the woods, Allison said, "I'll show you something better than that to check on."

After hearing Allison's story, Fred commented, "It seems that Teddy has some explaining to do. He may have been a little over anxious to collect on his inheritance." Fred tucked the flag in his shirt pocket.

"When Sam gets back, I'll send him out to take some pictures of the budding development. Let's go see what the others have found in the garage."

"Not much," Dominic replied to Fred's question. "There were some places on the floor where the dust had been disturbed like something might have been dragged. Hard to tell about footprints, probably most of them are ours. We'll see what the fingerprints show."

Gail spoke up, "No sign of the weapon. At least nothing with any blood on it. Though I don't know how anyone could have disposed of it so quickly."

"Of course, maybe it wasn't disposed of," Dominic said, his black eyes again probing into every corner of the garage. "There's all sorts of things here one could use to bash a head: lug wrench, piece of drain pipe, shovel. Just wipe the blood off and drop it down. Who would notice?"

"But then the assailant would have a bloody rag to dispose of," Allison said, "and that might be even harder." All three of the law officers looked at Allison in surprise. She laughed. "Hey, a little common sense goes a long way in this detective work."

It was close to an hour before a call came from the hospital. They were back in the house poking through hall closets and waste paper baskets. Fred picked up the phone on the second ring. "Yes?" He listened and nodded, listened and nodded. Allison was searching his face for some indication of the news. It revealed nothing. Finally he said, "Right," and hung up. Fred gave the others a reassuring smile.

"That was Sam. The doctor thinks the girl will make it, but it might be a while before she comes to. Then she may not remember anything."

"But she'll be all right? Normal?" Allison asked.

"Probably too early to tell. Sam says there were at least two blows to the head."

"So it couldn't have been an accident?" In the back of her mind, Allison still hadn't wanted to believe the alternative.

"No way."

Gail sighed. "Poor kid." She turned to Dominic. "Well, on to bigger and better things. I guess it's time to tackle the trash can by the back door. I think we have enough daylight left. I found some old newspapers. We can empty the contents on that."

As Dominic turned to go out, his rather large foot came down on a rather long tail. This was followed by a piercing howl and a blur of orange fur tearing down the hall. "What on earth was that?"

"That," Allison answered, "was Lancelot, who has no business being in the house. He has a habit of sneaking in whenever the door is opened." Allison coaxed the cat out from under a table and gently carried him outside. She walked slowly back into the house, her arms crossed, in deep thought. "I wonder who let Lancelot in that night?" she said to Fred.

"What night?"

"The night of the murder. I know he was outside after Catherine and I came in, but he was on the stairs when I came down for my run the next morning. No one else was up yet. Someone must have entered the lodge after we did and let him in."

Gail got out her little notebook and started flipping through the pages. "According to this all the others said they were in their rooms. You and Catherine were the last to come in."

"So all we have to do," Fred said, "is to figure out if one of the family lied or if someone else came in."

"Anyone could have, you know," Allison said. "These people don't believe in locking doors."

Gail and Dominic had just finished their trash can binge when Sam drove up. They'd found nothing to get excited about. Fred had pulled a dilapidated yard chair from the garage and was sitting in it, staring at the woods. Allison was sitting on the back steps praying for Becky, for Catherine, for the entire mess.

Sam came up to Fred to give his report. The others clustered around. "The doctor said, according to the wounds, the weapon was round, one or two inches in diameter, and probably metal. Most likely a piece of pipe. The girl has a small skull fracture. He doubts any permanent brain damage. She was starting to respond when I left the hospital.

"What about the family?" Fred asked. "Notice anything odd, out of character?"

"Not really. They're all pretty much shook up. There was one thing, though…."

"Yes?"

"It was the girl's father. When the doctor told her parents they could see her, he put his head on the bed rail, started sobbing and said, 'This wasn't supposed to happen.' Then he told her he loved her." Sam wiped sweat from his forehead. They were standing in the shade of a huge oak tree, but the early evening heat was intense. "It just seemed like a rather odd thing to say—almost like he was apologizing."

Fred nodded. "Indeed it does."

"There's another strange thing," Allison said. "Catherine told me something about the family meeting that Charles failed to mention when he was talking to you." Four pairs of eyes focused on Allison. Flustered, she started to stammer. "That is, well, I'm sure it's nothing." Allison took a deep breath. "When Bess announced she was going to sell the land to loggers, Charles said he wouldn't let her do it, that he would stop her somehow. What do you think he intended to do?"

Dominic said the words that Allison was thinking, "Maybe just what he did do—killed her before she could sign any papers."

"Something to ponder," Fred said. "Anyway there's nothing else we can do today. It's getting dark and I'm getting hungry. We'll get started again in the morning." He gave his instructions to the others. "Sam, you and Dominic check out the woods first thing tomorrow." He pulled the yellow flag from his pocket and told them of Allison's discovery. "See if you can find out what company this belongs to. And, Gail, you can take your trusty notebook and recheck everyone's statements. I'll go by the hospital before I come out."

Fred turned to Allison. "I don't like you staying

here by yourself. Gail could take you to a motel for the night and pick you up in the morning."

"Thanks, but I'll be fine. I'm sure some of the family will be coming home later." She managed a chuckle. "I'm a big girl now, you know. It's been a long time since I was afraid of the dark."

"It's not the dark," Fred said soberly. "It's who may be hiding in the dark." He scribbled something on a piece of paper. "My home phone. Call me if you need anything."

After everyone had left, Allison raided the refrigerator. There were plenty of leftovers, but she had little appetite. She dished out some potato salad, a few baked beans, and picked up a drumstick. She carried her plate and iced tea to the dining room, decided it was too lonely, and went to the library. Allison chose the same chair she had occupied when listening to the suspects make their statements. Although, at the time, they weren't actually suspects. Fred had been doing an unexpected death inquiry then, not a homicide investigation. She knew that if he had seriously believed the death to be murder, she would not have been privy to the conversations.

Daylight was fast fading and she turned on the desk lamp. Seeing some stationary and a pen, she picked them up. Now where did I leave my glasses? Allison had learned that the trouble with reading glasses was that she only needed them for reading, or for writing something she wanted to be able to read later. She needed them now, and of course, they were in her room where she'd left them when changing clothes after the funeral.

Allison reluctantly placed her plate on the coffee table and headed for the stairs. There was still enough light to see by, but eerie shadows clawed at her footsteps, and made her as jumpy as a jackrabbit. She hurried into her room, grabbed the glasses, and scooted back to the library. She took three deep breaths to calm herself, a technique she'd learn in a long-ago meditation class, and reclaimed her supper.

In between bites, Allison made a list of names. At first it was a short list: Charles, Teddy, Imogene, Derita. Then remembering Fred's admonition that no one was above suspicion, she reluctantly added: Catherine, Lillian, Serena, Jake, and last of all Paul. She smiled to herself and thought, if someone else was making this list he would place my name there too.

On top of the list Allison wrote, suspects/questions—discuss with Fred. Then concentrating on Bess's murder, she followed each name with notations.

Charles—threatened Bess? odd statement in hospital.

Teddy—making deal to develop land behind Bess's back? did he really go to kitchen when he left his room?

Imogene—knew of Teddy's dealings?

Derita—did she really hear Bess's voice at about 9:30?

Catherine—her disease? why did she lie?

Lillian—did she come back to the lodge night of murder?

Serena—ditto.

Jake—ditto. he was angry with Bess.

Paul—is he really who he says he is?

Other questions:

how was the cyanide administered? when?

what did Becky see or hear?

who let Lancelot in?

Allison studied the list, went back to Jake's name and added, *bought poison spray for fruit trees.* She knew there were other questions to be added, but she had run out of paper and out of patience. "This is driving me crazy. I've got to get out of here." Allison didn't know if she was talking to herself or to the ghost in the empty recliner. She wadded up the paper, tossed it toward the waste basket, missed her target, and decided to let it stay on the floor where it'd fallen. She dropped her glasses on the coffee table, hurried into the hall, and slammed out the front door. "I wish I'd gone to a motel for the night," she said. "I was a fool to stay here alone. Why did I have to act so brave? I guess I just wanted to impress Fred. Actually, I'm as scared as a lost puppy." Like many people who live alone, Allison had gotten into the habit of thinking out loud, asking herself questions and then answering them in the same breath. "I wish Catherine or Paul or somebody would come back. But what if the wrong person came back? And how would I know if it was the wrong person?" She fingered the paper with Fred's phone number.

"Maybe I should call him. And tell him—what? Admit that I'm afraid of the dark? Never!"

AFTER GETTING HOME, warming up some spaghetti he'd made the night before, riding his exercise bike, and watching an asinine sitcom, Fred still couldn't relax. He decided to go by the hospital and see for himself just what was going on.

It was late. He was told by a nurse that Becky was in and out of consciousness, her vital signs stable, the doctor encouraged. Fred spoke briefly to the young uniformed officer assigned to guard Becky. He was stationed outside her door, but made sure the door stayed opened so he had a clear view of his charge. He shook his head in answer to Fred's question of noticing anything suspicious. The family members appeared to ignore the officer's presence.

Fred supposed they were wondering what the lead detective was doing there, and frankly, Fred didn't know himself why he'd come. There was nothing he could do. Now was neither the place nor the time for further questioning, but maybe he could get a better feel for the family members.

Vera June and Charles were on either side of Becky's bed. Wesley had fallen asleep in the waiting room, his head on Derita's lap. Catherine and Paul hunched in a far corner. The officer told Fred that Teddy and Imogene had left a short while earlier.

Fred stepped into Becky's room, nodded to her parents and gazed at the tiny head wrapped like a mummy. *We'll find out who hurt you, Becky. I promise.* Although he had spoken to himself, Fred saw Vera June and Charles stare up at him. He had to say something. "I'm sure she'll be all right. I'll check with you in the morning."

As he left the room, he heard Vera June urge Charles to go back to the lodge. "There's no need for both us to stay here. Take Wesley back and let him get a good night's rest. Goodness knows, he needs it."

Charles nodded. He bent over, kissed the bandage of Becky's forehead, squeezed Vera June's hand. "I'll be back early. Call me if there's any change— if you need anything."

Fred watched as Charles tenderly lifted his son, letting Wesley's head rest on his broad shoulder. Paul pushed the elevator button. "I'll go down with you and help load him in the car."

He'd met Paul only briefly that afternoon, but hadn't had a chance to interview him about the murder. It could wait until tomorrow. For now, Fred simply wanted to watch and listen and think for a few minutes. He slumped on a hot vinyl couch close to the victim's door, and looked around the waiting area.

Derita stepped into Becky's room. "I'll stay if you want me to, Vera June."

"No, you and Catherine go. I'd really rather be alone with Becky."

"I understand. I think I'll stop by the motel and see Mom and Dad," Derita said. "I may get me a room there for the night."

When Paul came back up, he reported to Vera

June, "Charles put him in the back seat and Wesley didn't wiggle a muscle. I don't think an earthquake could wake that boy tonight."

Vera June gave a tired smile. "I know how he feels. The nurse is going to send a cot in for me to rest on. You take Catherine on home. She needs some sleep too."

Catherine wasn't convinced she should leave. "There's nothing else you can do here," Paul reminded her, "and you really shouldn't leave Allison alone any longer."

"I know you're right, although Allison's probably not alone now. Teddy and Imogene may already be there. In fact Teddy may at this very moment be in the kitchen up to his ears in peach cobbler." Fred noted that tears filled Catherine's eyes as she apparently realized what she'd just said. She wiped them away with shaking hands. "How can I make a joke at a time like this?"

"It's all right. This has been rough on you. You need to get some rest. Let's go." Paul slipped an arm around her waist as they waited for the elevator.

Fred guessed it was time for him to leave also. He stuck his head in for another look at Becky, signaled good-bye to Vera June, and got back to the elevator just in time to see the door slowly sliding shut. Both Catherine and Paul saw him, but neither made an effort to stop the door so he could join them. He shrugged and headed for the stairs. He didn't blame them for not wanting his company. He reached the parking lot shortly after they did.

Catherine was climbing into her car. "Sure you don't want to ride with me?" Paul said. "We could pick up your car in the morning." Catherine shook her head.

"Well, I'll be right behind you," Paul told her. He headed toward his pickup, and called back. "I forgot. I drove all the way here with the gas gauge on empty. I'll have to stop and fill up."

"That's fine," Catherine called back. "You don't have to follow me. Just go on home. You look like you've been through a war."

"You mean I don't look like a knight in shining armor anymore?"

"Better than that. You look like a friend."

ALLISON SAT ON THE PORCH for several minutes waiting for her nebulous fear to abate. It didn't. She stood up with resolution and made her way down the hill to the lake. It was pitch black now. The sun had long gone and the man in the moon hadn't yet shown his face, but Allison felt a deep need to be near the water. She'd always been enchanted by water. It didn't matter if it was lake, stream, ocean or pond. Being near the water made her feel close to God.

Years earlier when her husband had left her with two small children, she'd retreated to the beach for healing. She'd watch her children play in the sand, and sunlight dance on the waves. It had brought her comfort, strength and peace. Through the years it'd been the lakesides, the ponds, the creeks where she'd listened to God's reassurances. She needed that now.

Allison walked to the deep end of the pier and sat on the edge. She took off her shoes, wiggled her toes in the cool water, talked to herself and to God. Night sounds flickered in and out of her consciousness: a breeze stirring the weeping willow, happy crickets strumming with their legs, frogs sending messages across the waves. Her mind started writing a poem from the sounds. The process was soothing, assuaging her qualms.

Time passed. Calmness settled over her mind and her heart. She entered into a realm of meditation that blocked out all fears, all sounds—and all caution.

TEN

ALLISON FELT THE BLOW. In the moment before the world receded in nothingness, her head exploded with a spasm of pain. The next thing she felt was the chill of the water and slimy tentacles clawing at her face, choking her neck. Lakes had always been Allison's friends, now this one was the enemy—suffocating her, strangling her, doing its best to destroy her. But she couldn't let that happen. She flailed at the water, tried to disentangle her arms and legs from the clinging weeds.

Air. She needed air. She needed air now. Her head popped through the surface of the water only to be met by another blow, this time from the planks above her head. It was too dark to see anything, but Allison realized she must be trapped under the pier. She'd noticed earlier in the day that the boat dock was only a few inches above the water line. And when she toppled, *or was pushed,* into the lake she must have floated back under the dock.

She stifled a scream for help which tried to erupt from her throat. She knew it would bring no help, and would only alert her assailant that she was still alive. She had to get out, out from under the pier, out of the water. But she felt herself going woozy again, the darkness was streaked with weird, unreal lights emanating not from her surroundings, but from her battered brain. Her hands thrashed about, seeking something, anything, to grab.

She had to keep her head above the traitorous water. Her left hand collided with a narrow board. Her exploring fingers found a space between the board and the flooring of the pier which had become her prison. She managed to slip her wrist through the gap before the lights disappeared, and she again floated into an unknown galaxy.

The next time Allison rallied, the moon was beginning to shimmer on the water, turning the lake to a fantasy of sparkle and glitter. It took her a few moments to conclude that this time the brilliance was real. How much time had passed? She couldn't see the moon itself. Was it just emerging above the treetops on the opposite shore or was it already sailing at its apex? A chill shuddered through her body. The water temperature must have dropped several degrees since the heat of the day.

Her left wrist throbbed with pain, but she was afraid to pull it out. Her grasp on the board, which she now knew was a piling of the pier, was the only thing which had kept her from making like a submarine. She massaged the wrist with her other hand, restoring some circulation. Her eyes groped the water for clues to the direction of the shore. There were none. Her only hope was to release her hold on the piling and push herself one way or the other until she was out from under the pier. Then she could see where she was and swim to land. But before she could execute her plan, the lights inside her skull joined those made by the moon until she could no longer distinguish between the two and gave up the effort.

Allison awoke to the sound of splashing and humming. Who, she marveled, would be out here in the middle of the night, humming some hymn? She should know the song, but couldn't quite come up with the title. Or was this an angel greeting her at the pearly gates? If so, she hoped the angel had a giant size bath towel with him and a change of clothes. She wanted out of these wet things. She felt she ought to call out to whomever was there, but could manage only a low moan. She tried again. Her throat was parched. How can I be thirsty, she wondered, when I'm surrounded by water? This time the moan was louder and ended with a weak, "Help me."

The humming hushed. The splashing stopped. A voice, a masculine human voice, called out, "Who's there?" And then, "Where are you?"

Allison thought she recognized the voice, but her mind wouldn't give him a name. It didn't matter. It was a kind voice, one she could trust. She swallowed hard and forced the words out, "Over here, the pier." The effort was too much. Her brain floated away again as the words floated across the water.

PAUL TURNED TOWARD the sound, his eyes probing the dark water where the moonlight had not yet penetrated. "Where?" he pleaded. "Speak to me." He stood still, listening for any sound, any sign. There was nothing. The words had been so low, he wasn't sure if it was a woman's voice or a child's, but somebody needed help. He made his way toward the pier, found its edge and walked out into the lake as far as he could. When his feet could no longer touch bottom, he swam out keeping the pier to his right. He kept calling out, but there was no answer. When he reached the end of the pier, he dove under and fumbled in the blackness like a blind man in unfamiliar territory. His hands found only empty water.

His foot felt the body first. He grabbed wildly, feeling for a face. He found it. It was still above water. Maybe his eyes had become accustomed to the dark or perhaps the moon had risen just enough to extend under the pier, but the face's features came into focus. "Allison?"

He enveloped her face with his hands, intermittently shaking and patting it, while thrashing his feet to keep himself afloat. "Allison, wake up. Do you hear me? Wake up!"

Allison woke up, opened her eyes, smiled, and promptly passed out again. Paul cradled her head in the crook of his right elbow while he tried to extricate both of them from their watery prison. His first task was to pry loose her arm which was twisted around a piling. He was finally able to release her wrist and when he did, Allison started to sink. Paul grabbed her around the neck from behind to keep her nose and mouth out of the water. The wooden pier was only inches above their heads. He had to keep his own head bent down while trying to maneuver Allison out. When he got her out to the open water, it was a simple matter to haul her to the shore. Once there, he made sure she was breathing and then wasted no more time trying to revive her. Instead, he placed one arm under her knees, the other behind her back and carried her, as he would a child, up the steep slope.

When he reached the porch, he gently laid her down. She opened her eyes and started shivering. "Cold. So cold," she croaked.

Paul opened the front door and ran into the house. "Thank God they don't lock doors around here," he muttered. He started for the back stairs, hollering as he ran. "Catherine! Charles! Teddy! Come quick. Allison needs your help."

Catherine met him at the top of the stairs. "What's the matter?"

"Allison's been hurt. Wake the others. I need help getting her into the house." He started back downstairs. "And bring a blanket."

Catherine asked no questions. She slammed into Charles's room, demanded he follow her, grabbed a blanket from the closet shelf, and nearly tripped as she tore down the stairs. Charles ran after her, rubbing his eyes, pulling on a tee shirt.

Catherine covered her friend with a blanket, then held the door open as Charles and Paul carried Allison into the house. "The library couch," Catherine directed. When the men laid their burden down,

Allison shook her head as if trying to clear out the cobwebs and shivered.

Catherine took charge. "We've got to get those wet clothes off. Charles, get the robe that's lying on my bed and some more blankets. Paul, heat some water and make her tea. You'll find tea bags on the counter." Paul hesitated. He didn't even know where the kitchen was. Catherine pointed. "Through there. Light switch on left. Counter on right."

Paul followed her directions, but turned back to ask, "And where can I find a towel? I'm dripping all over the place."

Catherine smiled. "Actually, the wet tee shirt look becomes you, but I'll have Charles bring you something to change into. There are towels in the hall closet—that way."

"Thanks. By the way, where's Teddy and Imogene? They left the hospital before we did."

"I found a note on my bedroom door from Teddy. He said they decided to go back to town and spend the night at a motel. Charles and Wesley must have been sleeping when I came in and I assumed that Allison was too. I guess I should have checked her room, but I just wanted to get to bed."

"There was no reason for you to check on her. As late as it was, you'd have expected her to be asleep. You can't blame yourself for anything." Paul went in hunt of a towel and then headed for the kitchen.

Catherine had Allison stripped under the blanket when Charles and Paul returned. "Help her sit up, Charles, while I get this robe on her." Having accomplished this task, Catherine replaced the damp blanket with two dry ones.

ALLISON REENTERED the land of the living with the purr of a happy cat. "Feels good," she managed to say. She rubbed her throat, "Water?"

Charles hurried to fetch her a glass of water. A few gulps and she was finally able to talk. "Thanks. Now if you could squash this pounding in my head, I'd be indebted to you for life."

"I heard that. And I have the cure. Hot tea and aspirin." Paul sat down the tray with both items on it, plus the sugar bowl and some saltines. "Life in this household must be full of headaches, seeing that the aspirin occupies an honored spot next to the coffee pot." Allison bolted the aspirin, sipped the tea and nibbled a cracker.

Charles, Paul and Catherine pulled up chairs and watched her. After a little bit, Catherine asked, "Feel like telling us what happened?"

"I don't know what happened. One minute I was deep in meditation and the next minute I was deep in cold water. In between I was bashed on the head."

"Bashed?" Charles asked. "You sure you didn't just trip and fall into the lake."

"It's pretty hard to trip when you're sitting down. Someone hit me on the head. Then I either fell or was pushed into the water. The blow knocked me out. The water woke me up. I grabbed hold of a board and then kind of vacillated between this world and the next for goodness knows how long." Allison looked over to Paul. "I want to thank you for saving my life, but, if you don't mind me asking, what in the world were you doing down there at this hour of the night?"

"Rescuing my pontoon. After I got home, I remembered that I hadn't docked it. Catherine and I had jumped off when we heard Becky had been found. I did have enough presence of mind at the time to throw out the anchor, but I was afraid it might not hold it long enough."

"And another thing," Allison added, "what was the song you were humming? I couldn't think of the name."

Paul grinned. "I'm not sure that I recall. Depending on my mood, I usually hum either 'Dixie' or 'Beulah Land.' Of course, some people think the two lands are synonymous, so it doesn't really matter."

"Oh, it was definitely 'Beulah Land,'" Allison said. "I remember now because I thought it might be an angel welcoming me to my heavenly home." She started to laugh at the memory, then winced as a pain raced through her head.

Catherine got up. "Where does it hurt?"

"All over, but mostly right there," Allison said, as she rubbed the back of her head.

Feeling the place where Allison pointed, Catherine nodded. "No wonder. You've got a knot the size of New York."

"I'll get some ice to put on it," Charles said. "But why on earth would anyone want to hurt you?"

"The same reason someone tried to kill Becky. We know something that points to the murderer."

"And what is that?" Catherine asked. The three of them waited for her answer.

"I'll tell Detective Sawyer in the morning. Right now I'm going to take that ice bag and go to bed."

Paul shook his head, "Don't you think you should be checked out at the hospital—x-rays and all that? You might have a concussion."

"I'll be fine. I'm known for my hard head. And I'm not the least bit dizzy. All I need now is some sleep. I'll tell my story in the morning." Allison stared at the three people staring at her. They're dying from curiosity, she thought, but for my own safety I'd better not say anything else. From her place on the library couch, she'd noticed the paper listing names and questions was missing from the corner where she had thrown it. Her mind whirled with problems which this posed. Who had found it and read it? Whoever it was, would know she had written it since she was the only one here at the lodge. Which clue was the incriminating one? Had the list of suspects been narrowed down to these three? Catherine had said that Imogene and Teddy had been at the lodge earlier. When was that? When had Charles arrived? She was beginning to develop a severe case of paranoia. Had that really been aspirin Paul had shoved at her? Her headache was lessening, but she was beginning to get drowsy. Was that normal? And the worse thought of all—was Catherine a friend or a fiend? Allison struggled up from the couch. "I hear my bed calling to me. Good night, y'all."

Paul helped her up the stairs, Catherine tucked her in, Charles placed the ice bag on her head. Allison felt a flush of shame. They're all so nice to me, she thought. How can I suspect any of them? She was too tired to worry anymore. Her last conscious thought was: if I'm still alive in the morning, I'll discuss everything with Fred, and if I'm not, at least I'll have a good long rest.

ELEVEN

MORNING CAME. Allison was still alive. She awoke with no pain, a clear mind, and a ravenous appetite. She dressed quickly and remembered that Fred's home phone number was in her wet clothes. She hurried down the hall. Catherine's door was open, the room empty. Allison glimpsed a piece of stationery on the bedside table. It was the same color Allison had used the night before. Afraid of what she might find, she picked it up and was relieved to see it was not the list she had written. By extending her arm to its full length, she was able read the note without her glasses. It was the one that Teddy had left for Catherine. *We came by to get a change of clothes. Spending night at motel. T.*

Allison's forehead furrowed in deep thought. At least now she was sure there were more than three suspects in her attack. "And," she said aloud, "I wonder where dear Derita was when I was taking my midnight swim?"

Allison found Catherine, Charles, and Wesley in the kitchen. "It's everybody for themselves this morning," Charles explained. "Apparently Serena figured her job here was terminated. There's plenty of food, though. Help yourself."

"Thanks. I will. Have you heard from the hospital yet?"

"I just called," Charles said. "Becky is awake, but she can't remember anything. It's probably just as well."

Just as well for whom? Allison wondered, as she dropped a piece of whole wheat bread in the toaster.

Wesley crammed the last of his jelly doughnut in his mouth, swiped his hand across his lips and said excitedly, "I talked to Mommy. Becky's going to be okay. She said we could go home pretty soon."

Catherine got up and gave Wesley a hug. "It won't be long before you and your sister can start fighting and arguing again."

Wesley grinned. "Yeah. That's what big sisters are for."

"You all right?" Catherine asked Allison. "You gave us quite a scare last night."

"I'm fine. I need the clothes I had on last night. Are they still in the library?"

"No. I draped them over the washing machine." Catherine pointed toward the back of the kitchen. "In the utility room. Don't worry about them. I'll do a load of laundry after a while. I have some wet clothes to wash, too."

"I just need to get something out of the pocket." Allison came back with a slip of paper in her hand. "I'm going to see if I can catch Fred before he leaves home."

FRED SHOOK HIS HEAD as Allison described her harrowing experience. He called Gail, reported into the office, then called the hospital to check on Becky's condition. He wolfed breakfast and was soon on his way to the Blue Goose. Paul walked up as Fred drove in. Allison, who had been waiting on the back steps, greeted both of them. The men nodded warily at each other.

Paul spoke first, "I hope you've got a handle on this nasty business. We could have lost Allison last night."

Fred winced. "We'll get to the bottom of it. Trust me." He turned to Allison. "Are you sure you're all right?"

Allison attempted a smile. "Still a wee bit shook up, but I'll survive."

"I need all the details, when it happened, who was here, who wasn't accounted for, and why you didn't call me immediately."

"I don't know when it happened," Allison replied. "Sometime after dark and before Paul found me, which I understand was sometime after midnight. I know Gail isn't going to like that answer, but it's the best I can do. As to who was here at one time or another—that would be Teddy, Imogene, Charles, Wesley, and Catherine."

"And me," Paul put in.

"And Paul, my rescuer. I don't know where Jake or Lillian or Serena or Derita was. And the best answer to why didn't I call you immediately is—I wasn't up to it and there would have been nothing you could have done anyway."

"You should have let me be the judge of that,"

Fred growled. He looked up as Catherine joined them. "Who all is here right now?" he asked her.

"Just us three, Paul and Allison and me," Catherine answered. "Charles and Wesley went back to the hospital. The others spent the night in town. Teddy called and said he had to get back to Charlotte. He's been trying to get in touch with you."

"Call him back and tell him to get his tail out here. He needs to clear up a couple of things. Of course, I'm not detaining anybody," Fred added hastily. "Just asking for cooperation." Another sheriff's car drove up. "Here's Gail now. Let's find a nice cool spot and talk. And I wouldn't turn down a cup of coffee if there's any available."

Fred thought the library would be the natural place for questions and answers. Catherine brought in a coffee pot and five cups. Fred placed five chairs in a circle around the coffee table. Gail got out her notebook. "Now we'll get to work," Fred said. "Allison, you start."

Allison started with everything that had happened after Fred had left the evening before. She told about the list of suspects, of tossing it away, of going down to the lake, of sitting, of meditating, of writing poetry in her head, of the bashing and the aftermath. Gail scribbled furiously.

When she finished, Fred asked, "Are you sure your list of questions and clues is now missing?"

Allison pointed to the waste basket. "It was on the floor there. It isn't now."

"Right. We'll get back to that." Fred turned to

Catherine. "Your turn. If you don't mind answering a couple of questions. What were your movements? And tell me what you know about what your cousins were doing."

Fred knew he was walking a fine line between gathering information and questioning suspects. He just wished he knew which cousin to zero in on.

"You know when everybody left the hospital. You were there," Catherine said. Fred nodded. Catherine went on, "I came on home. Charles's car was parked by the back door. He and Wesley were sleeping. I was surprised not to see Teddy's car and then I found the note he'd written. And of course, I figured Allison had gone to bed hours earlier.

"Paul had offered to follow me home, but I told him it wasn't necessary. So he drove directly back to his travel trailer. You know he has to take a different road to get down to that point of land. It takes more time to drive there from here than it does to walk. And I'm sure you heard Derita say she was going to stay in town. That's about it." Catherine looked at Paul. "Did I leave anything out?"

"I think that about covers it," Paul said. "Except we don't know for sure that Charles was sleeping. And we don't know just when Teddy and Imogene were here, or what time he left the note. Not that it really matters."

"It may," Fred said. "We'll check that out later, but tell us now just how you found Allison."

When Paul finished his story, he added, "I don't know how I had the strength to carry her up the hill, but thank God I was able to do it."

"Yes, indeed," Fred said. "And thank God you went down to see about your boat." Allison and Catherine smiled in agreement. "When Sam and Dominic get here," Fred said, "I'll have them search the area for a weapon. Doubt if they'll find anything, though."

Fred poured another cup of coffee, stirred in three teaspoons of sugar and turned back to Allison. "Now about that list of yours—I want you to rewrite it as exactly as possible. No improvising—exact word for word."

Allison closed her eyes so she could better visualize what she had written. "Gail, maybe it would be easier if I dictated it to you. I think I can recall it better that way."

"Sure," the detective replied, pencil poised. "Ready when you are."

Gail recorded Allison's words as Fred, Catherine, and Paul listened attentively. When she came to Jake's name, she asked Fred, "Do they put cyanide in poison sprays nowadays?"

"Maybe," Fred answered. "We'll check it out."

When the dictation ended, Catherine spoke up. "I think I can answer one of those questions."

The others waited. "Well, go ahead," Fred urged. "Which one?"

"About Lancelot. It must have been Charles who let the cat inside. You see, Charles wasn't in the house when Allison and I came in."

Gail flipped back a few pages in her notebook. "But he said he'd gone to bed early."

"Then he must have gone out again. I peeked in the children's rooms before going to bed. Becky was asleep, but Wesley was awake and told me he'd heard voices outside his window. He was scared, and when I asked him why he hadn't gotten his dad, he said he looked in his dad's room and it was empty. I thought at the time Wesley had imagined the voices, but maybe the boy was right."

"Wesley did seem scared," Allison said. "I was just outside the door and I heard him tell Cat his dad wasn't in bed."

"It might be Charles slipped out to meet someone," Fred said. "But who and why? Seems like several people haven't been completely honest with us." Catherine stared at the floor as if finding the wood grain suddenly fascinating.

Paul broke the ensuing silence. "I'd like to reply to the comment after my name. It would be easy enough for you to validate my story—find out if I'm for real."

"I know," Fred said. "I already have. You *are* a minister. Your wife *was* killed in an accident. You *are* on vacation. And there's no indication you had ever met Bess Lattimer."

Allison gave Paul an imploring look. "I'm sorry. It's not that I didn't believe you. I just didn't want to leave anybody out."

"It's all right. No hard feelings."

"There are two others on your list, Allison, that we can eliminate in Bess's murder," Gail said. "Lillian and Serena have alibis for that evening.

Lillian was playing bingo at All Saint's Church. She won some pot holders and Chantilly cologne. Serena was studying for an exam with two friends. Neither one left for home until after eleven, by which time Bess was probably already dead."

"There's one more thing on the list we need to discuss before moving on," Fred said. Allison, Paul, and Gail looked at him. Catherine didn't. "I think you need to clear up something for us, Catherine."

Catherine looked up. "Me?"

"I didn't catch it myself, but Allison thinks you lied about wanting to donate money for cancer research. Do you want to change your story?"

Catherine sat up straight, held her head up high, almost looked defiant and said to her friend, "What makes you think I lied?"

"I'm sorry, Cat, but I could tell. Your answer was too smooth, too practiced."

"So you want the truth?" Catherine shoved her chair back, put her hands on her hips and glared at each of them in turn. No one blinked. "All right. I'll tell you the truth and I hope it makes you happy!" Catherine held out her hands. They were trembling like tree limbs caught in a twister. "This is my disease!"

Allison, Paul, Gail and Fred all stared in puzzlement at Catherine, waiting for her to explain. She did. "I have Huntington's chorea. You may have never heard of it. It's a neurological disease. It's hereditary. It's incurable. It's hellish."

None of the four took their eyes off the narrator.

It was as if they were holding their collective breaths. Fred was almost afraid to hear more, but he needed to hear more. Maybe this was the breakthrough he'd been waiting for.

More came. "It will slowly destroy my mind and my body. It has already destroyed my past and my future." Catherine blinked back tears. "It was a gift from my mother."

She clenched her hands together, but they continued to quiver. Her voice dropped to a whisper. "My mother killed herself because of it. She also killed my father, and tried to kill me."

Gail's pencil fell to the floor; she made no motion to pick it up. Fred wiped invisible sweat off his forehead. Paul bowed his head and his lips moved silently. Allison reached out to touch her friend, but Catherine stepped back.

"Aunt Bess was a very generous person." Catherine's voice became loud and shrill, the corners of her mouth rigid with hatred. "She gave me two gifts for my college graduation: a new car and the horrifying truth about my mother and my legacy from her. I knew Mama had been sick, but I didn't know with what or how bad. I remember her shaking hands, her slurred speech, her crying in frustration. I remember Daddy trying to console her and telling me not to worry. And I remember that day: our car plunging into the river, their silence, my screaming. I was in the back seat and the back of the car stuck out of the water. I was able to hold my head above the water until I was rescued." Catherine turned her head and looked at the still water of the lake. "There's been so many times I've wished I'd drowned with them. The police told me it had been an accident and that's what I believed until Aunt Bess told me differently.

"I can still hear her voice. It was like she'd been wanting to tell me the story for years, just waiting for the right time to ravage my life. She said, *'It was your mother who was driving that day. I can't imagine why your father let her drive, but he did. The whole thing was deliberate. She wanted to put an end to her nightmare and take her family with her. Maybe she thought she was doing you a favor—so you wouldn't have to live through the hell she had. Well, her plan didn't work. She took my brother with her, but left her kid for me to care for.'"*

Tears trickled down Catherine's cheeks. "Her words kept slapping me in the face. *'You have her genes, you know. Sooner or later the symptoms will show up.'* I thought she might be wrong. Only fifty percent of children inherit the Huntington gene. I thought maybe I would be one of the lucky ones. I took the test. But she'd been right, just like she was right about everything else."

Catherine shoved her hands into her pockets. "So yes, I lied. I wanted my share of her money for research on this damnable curse. I thought it might help someone else, although it's too late to help me. Until now I never told anyone else of her revelation to me. I didn't want my cousins' pity. And I was afraid if people knew, I might not be able to get a job or any insurance." She looked directly at Allison. "If that lie gives me a motive for murder, so be it."

Catherine fled the room, banging out the front door. Allison rose to go after her; Paul motioned her back. He caught up with Catherine on the porch steps and they headed down to the lake together.

Allison went to the window, watched them as they walked out on the pier. "We shouldn't have done that to her," she said. "It was cruel."

"It couldn't be helped." Fred came over and joined Allison at the window. "We have to turn over every stone in our search for the truth. That's what being a detective is all about. Sometimes innocent people get hurt. It happens that way."

"I don't like being a detective," Allison cried.

"It's too late to back out now. The murderer knows that you know something, and you're a danger to him or her. You won't be safe until this case is solved."

"But I don't know what I know. The clues are there, the questions are there, but what do they mean?"

"It'll come to us. You or Gail or I or somebody will have a sudden flash and then we'll know. We'll know the murderer!"

TWELVE

Catherine and Paul climbed on the pontoon and pushed away from the pier. Dominic and Sam arrived and started exploring along the shore. Fred made a call to the hospital and then reported to Allison. "Becky's awake and talking. I think my next step is to hear what she has to say." He asked Gail to stay at the lodge until Catherine came back in and make sure she was all right. He couldn't erase the thought of her mother's desperate act. He hated that they'd had to dig up the painful past. This murder investigation was having too many victims.

"You want me to go with you?" Allison asked.

Fred shook his head and then grinned as Allison dropped her eyes to the floor. He reached out and tilted her chin up. "On second thought, I think you'd better come. I don't want you getting into any more trouble."

"Suits me."

Becky was indeed awake, talking, and most importantly, remembering. She was telling her story to her family, most of whom had returned to the hospital. Other than Catherine, all the cousins stood there hovering over Becky's every word. The officer on guard hadn't received orders to exclude any visitors, but he stayed alert and watchful. Fred arrived at the same time as Becky's pediatrician. The doctor politely asked everyone to leave the room, then motioned for Fred to follow him in. Fred, in turn, escorted Allison into the room. After his examination, the doctor indicated Fred could question the girl.

"Now, Becky, can you tell us exactly what happened?"

Becky was eager to comply. "I was just walking around, waiting for Mommy to say it was time to go. I wanted to go home. It was sad around there after the funeral. I found a golf ball in the grass and kicked it with my foot. It hit the side of the garage. I went to kick it again and saw the side garage door was open a little. So I went in. It was kind of dark and spooky, and I didn't like it in there. I started to go out when I saw a squirt bottle in the corner and started to pick it up."

"And why did you want the squirt bottle?"

"I know," Wesley piped up. He'd sneaked back into the room and was eager for his say. "She was going to put water in it and squirt people."

"Only one person, Smarty. I was going to squirt you." Becky glared at her brother and then looked back at Fred. "So I bent down to pick it up and that's all I remember."

"You don't remember getting hit?"

"No."

"Did you hear anything?"

"I don't think so."

"Did you see anything else? Anybody?"

"I'm not sure. When I bent over, I think I saw someone or something, but I can't remember just what it was—maybe it was just a shadow. I keep trying to remember, but I can't."

"Do you remember just what the bottle looked like?"

"Sure. Small, white, with a nozzle."

Allison gulped. "The nasal spray. Fred, it has to be the nasal spray bottle."

"We can find out easily enough," the doctor said. "We'll have the pharmacist send one up. Maybe Becky can identify it."

"Good girl." Fred patted Becky on the arm. "You've been a big help."

Fred followed the doctor out of the room. "She's going to be fine then?"

"Looks like it. Kids are resilient. The mother wants to take her home."

"Are you going to let her go?"

"I see no reason not to. But I'd like her to go by ambulance with a nurse in attendance, in case there are any delayed reactions. That all right with you, Mr. Sawyer?"

"Yes. But don't let any family member, except her mother, be alone with her—not before she goes and not in the ambulance." The doctor looked at Fred quizzically, but didn't ask questions.

Allison sat in the waiting room studying the little girl's family. Fred slid into a seat next to her. "A penny for your thoughts."

"The assailant is right in this room," she said. "The person who killed Bess and tried to kill Becky and me is in this very room."

"Probably."

Before Allison could say anything else, Teddy came up to Fred, trailed by Derita and Charles. "Now look here, Mr. Sawyer," Teddy said, "I understand your situation, but I've got a business to run. How much longer are we going to be held hostage?"

"You're not being held hostage. You're free to go. However, I'm sure you want to get to the bottom of this case as much as I do. So it would help if I could get some honest answers from you and the others. Shall we meet back at the lodge and finish the questioning?"

"Surely this won't take much longer," Derita said. "My fiancé is expecting me at home, and frankly I can't see what else we can do here. Becky is going to be all right and Allison looks fine." Derita smiled at Allison. "Charles told me about your near escape. How terrible. Is it possible you simply went to sleep while you were meditating and fell into the water? Then maybe struck your head on the pier? I've fallen asleep before while meditating after my yoga session. It's so relaxing."

Allison wasn't going to argue with her. "I suppose it could have happened that way."

"Well, whatever happened she certainly gave us a scare," Charles said. "Did you find any clues this morning, Fred, which might explain it?"

"Not really, but we're still looking. We'll find the

answers, you know—to everything. It's just a matter of time." Fred stood up and stretched. "I've a few loose ends to tie up here and then I'll be back to the Blue Goose. I hope all of you will be there, too."

"Yes, Sir," Derita said, with a slight pout. "Allison can ride out with me if she wishes."

Fred spoke up before Allison had a chance to answer. "No," he said. "I need Allison's help a little longer. We'll be out shortly."

After the others left, Fred turned to Allison. "The same goes for you that I said about Becky."

Allison gave him a puzzled look. "What?"

"I don't want you to be alone with any of the suspects until this case is solved. You understand?" Allison nodded slowly.

The hospital pharmacist had checked with Dr. Caldwell, got the name of the nasal spray Bess Lattimer used and sent up a bottle for Becky's inspection. "That looks like it. Take off the cap," she said. Fred took off the cap revealing the spray nozzle. "Yeah, that's the kind of bottle it was. I'm pretty sure."

"But where does that get us?" Allison asked after they'd said good-bye to Becky. "We can't prove the poison was put in Bess's nasal spray if we don't find the bottle. And if it was, we still don't know who did it or when. And what was it doing in the garage?"

Fred pushed the elevator button. He was deep in thought. "But her spray bottle wasn't missing. We found it with her other medications."

"Maybe it was switched," Allison said. "That's it.

The murderer put poison in the bottle, used it to kill Bess and then switched it with another bottle. Remember there wasn't a nasal spray in the box of medications which had just been filled at the pharmacy."

When the elevator door opened Fred was so engrossed in his thoughts he didn't realize it was going up rather than down. He and Allison squeezed in next to a young man carrying red roses and a balloon announcing, *It's a boy!*

Fred smiled at him, shook his free hand and said, "Congratulations and good luck."

"Thanks," the man said. "I'll need all the luck I can get. It's kind of scary. Our first one."

"You'll do fine," Fred assured him. "Kids are wonderful. They can be a lot of trouble, but the joy they bring is worth it."

The new father grinned. "You're right. Thanks."

When the elevator emptied, Allison pushed the ground button and quizzed her companion. "What do you know about kids?"

"I love kids. Of course, never having any of my own makes that easy to say."

"Well, I agree that kids are wonderful. I have two, both in college now. But it wasn't easy raising them alone."

"Alone?"

"Their father took off years ago."

"I'm sorry."

"It's okay. We made it."

Fred waited for her to say something else, but

Allison apparently wasn't ready for a tell-all. Instead she said, "Speaking of good luck, I think we need some on this case."

"I've got a news flash for you, Allison. Luck doesn't solve crimes. It's just hard work and persistence." The elevator door opened and they exited.

Allison was swallowed by the revolving door while Fred pushed his way through the handicap exit. "Never could stand those things," he explained when Allison emerged.

"You don't like merry-go-rounds either?"

"You got that right. I go around in circles enough without doing it voluntarily."

THEIR NEXT STOP WAS the sheriff's office. Fred ushered Allison past the front desk, down a long hall, to the last door on the right. "My home away from home," he said proudly.

Allison liked what she saw. It wasn't spacious, but it was roomy enough for a large desk, a swivel chair complete with a red plaid cushion, several file cabinets, a computer table, three straight chairs, and a table holding a coffee maker and several packs of Nabs. The calendar on the wall displayed a picture of Glen Canyon Dam and on the opposite wall was a map of the county. Another wall held framed certificates and group pictures of uniforms and smiles.

Fred motioned Allison to sit down at his desk. "I need you to make a call to Derita's parents. They left early this morning and should be home by now."

"And tell them what?"

"You're not going to tell them anything. You're going to ask what time Derita was with them last night. Make up some excuse why you need to know."

"Such as?"

"You'll think of something. Use your imagination."

"And just why do we need to know?"

"Come on, Allison. I thought you were getting to know this detective game. The question is: where was Derita when you were getting bashed in the head?" Fred gave Allison a sly grin. "We already know she wasn't in her motel room."

"How do we know that?"

"I asked the desk clerk. Derita didn't check in until nearly one a.m." Allison shuddered remembering the cold water and reached for the phone. Fred handed her a piece of paper. "Here's the number."

"Mrs. Lattimer, this is Allison Aldridge. We met briefly yesterday at the funeral…. Yes, it was certainly a lovely service…. I'm sure she'll be greatly missed…. I know Derita was very fond of her aunt but, Mrs. Lattimer, the reason I'm calling is to ask if Derita left a book of mine in your motel room. I hate to disturb you at a time like this, but it's a valuable book and I had loaned it to Derita and she can't remember where she left it. I guess in all the confusion she just misplaced it, and…Yes, I know Derita loves to read. That's why I loaned her the book. But you see, I'm leaving in the morning and I need to find it. She had it with her at the hospital and I thought she might have left it in your room. What time did she come there?… I see. Well, thank you anyway. I'm sure it will show up somewhere. Bye now."

Allison slowly replaced the receiver and looked at Fred. "Isn't that interesting? It seems that Derita didn't stop in to see her parents at all after she left the hospital. They last saw her about eight o'clock when they went up to check on Becky. Her mother said they told Derita they were going to go to bed early, so they could catch their flight this morning."

"So again comes the question," Fred said, "where was Derita when you were taking your midnight swim? She left the hospital about eleven, checked into the motel two hours later. It's a forty-minute round trip to the Blue Goose."

Allison felt the receding bump on the back of her head. "That was a mighty hefty blow for a woman as small as she is."

"She works out. Remember? Aerobics and stuff." Fred put his hands on his hips and glanced down to where his stomach was overriding his belt. "Something I need to get back to."

"So our suspect list hasn't changed?"

"Except for Jake." Fred picked up a report from his desk. "The men I sent out this morning found no trace of our poison. The bug spray he bought was there, but no cyanide in it." Fred sat in a chair opposite Allison. "And although he has no alibi after he left the lodge about eight, it's unlikely he came back. Like he said, it's too far to walk through the woods and if he had rowed back, you people on the pontoon would no doubt have seen him."

"Well, I'm glad he's cleared," Allison said. "I've gotten to rather like the old buzzard."

Fred paused as he finished reading the report. "And it seems there's no cyanide at the Blue Goose either. No cyanide in anything: the garage, house, boathouse, the whole shebang. And there was none found in the food or any of the medications."

"Except possibly the missing nasal spray bottle." Allison twirled around in Fred's swivel chair. "Hey, this is fun. And you said you didn't like going around in circles." Allison went around again. "It helps me think." She abruptly stopped the chair, banged her hand on the desk and nearly shouted, "I know how Bess was killed!"

Fred sat on the edge of the desk and leaned his face close to Allison. "And how was that?"

"She killed herself. Not suicide. I mean the murderer let her kill herself." Allison was excited, twisting back and forth in the chair as she went on to explain. "I had been picturing the murderer holding the bottle to Bess's face and forcing the poison on her, but that's not the way it happened at all. The cyanide was placed in the bottle earlier, then the culprit left it on the table along with her other medications. He, or she, probably knew Bess used it every night before going to sleep. But what Bess inhaled that night was not her medicated spray; it was the cyanide. You told me it could be absorbed through the skin and some of it could have gotten to the lungs. It may not have taken much to kill her since her lungs were in such bad shape anyway. She thrashed about with her last breaths. That's why the medicine bottles and her pillow were on the floor. She may have called out for help, but no one heard her. Then sometime during the night, the murderer slipped into the room, took out the poisoned bottle and replaced it with another one. Then he, or she, hid the bottle somewhere, or threw it out the window, retrieved it the next day, and hid it in the garage until it could be disposed of properly."

Fred kept nodding his head throughout the recital. Allison thought he was beginning to look like a toy dog her son once loved who kept bobbing his head up and down. "The window," Fred said.

"The window?" Allison echoed.

"Derita said she went in to close her aunt's window, but it was already closed. We've got to check that window when we get back to the lodge. The bottle was still dangerous so the murderer may have thrown it out the window where it most likely landed in the grass."

"And the label became loose because it lay in the damp air all night."

"Exactly," Fred said. "But where would the infamous bottle be now?"

Allison twirled around in the chair one more time and came up with the answer. "At the hospital. In a trash can. What better place to dispose of a medicine bottle? The problem is that by now it's in a Dumpster along with all the other hospital waste. Gone forever."

"Not necessarily. Let's suppose, as you say, the

murderer took the bottle to the hospital and while in the waiting room, pretending concern about Becky's fate, wrapped the bottle in a tissue and dropped it in a waste paper basket." Now it was Allison's turn to do the nodding in agreement as Fred went on, "That would have been last evening and the housekeeping personnel probably emptied the trash first thing this morning."

Allison threw up her hands. "So it's gone."

"May I finish?" Fred asked politely. "It's *my* case, you know?"

"Sorry. Please go ahead."

"The waste baskets are emptied, but their contents don't go into the same container as the contaminated hospital wastes. In other words, the blood and guts are incinerated while the harmless trash awaits delivery to the landfill. Since it's rather a small hospital, they don't pick up daily. So chances are, the murder weapon is still there and all we need to do is find it." Fred picked up the phone and gave some unlucky underling the assignment.

"Of course," Allison said, "if they do find the bottle, and it does have traces of cyanide in it, we still don't know where the poison came from or who put it there."

"One step at a time, partner. One step at a time." Fred thought Allison blushed when he referred to her as his partner. He wondered if she liked the idea as much as he did.

THIRTEEN

ALLISON NOTICED DOMINIC sitting on the back stoop when she and Fred pulled up to the lodge. The officer was halfway to their car before Fred stopped and got out. "We may have found it, Sir," Dominic said. He held up a piece of galvanized pipe in a plastic bag. Allison came around the car and stood at Fred's elbow so she could get a good look. The pipe was about eighteen inches long, threaded at one end. "It was buried in the sand close to the pier, but part of it was visible. Probably hidden in a hurry. Looked like a stick at first, but Sam scratched around it with his knife and hauled it out." He handed his prize to Fred. "Probably no prints, but you never know."

Fred studied the pipe, held it up to the light for better viewing while a slow smile crossed his face. "Maybe we are getting some of that luck you were wishing for, Allison." Allison came closer as Fred took a pen out of his pocket and pointed. "Here, in this groove, a strand of hair and maybe flecks of blood."

"But I just got a bump on the head. I didn't bleed any," Allison said.

Dominic's head jerked up. "The little girl did.

The lab got a sample of her hair and blood at the hospital and we'll need a sample of your hair also, Ma'am. Chances are the same person used the same weapon in both attacks."

"But who?" Allison's head ached with the suspects' faces, the clues, the spray bottle, the cyanide—all chasing each other in her thoughts. "Who could have committed murder and attempted two others? It seems so unreal."

"Maybe we'll get some more answers when we go over their stories again," Fred said. "Where's Gail? And what about the others?"

"Gail's talking with Lillian in the kitchen," Dominic answered. "I think the rest are packing to leave. They're an anxious bunch."

"I imagine so, and at least one of them has reason to be." Fred dismissed the officer with a nod of his head and turned to Allison. "Let's check out that window in Bess's room, and then we'll get back to the questioning."

The yellow crime tape was still in place. The window was still closed and the room was stifling in the afternoon heat. Air conditioning had never made it to the old-fashioned lodge. Fred carefully examined the window and the sill. Then he slipped on a pair of gloves, slowly raised the window and peered out. Allison was right behind him. She noticed the bottom of the screen was pushed out. Fred stuck his hand through the opening. "The murderer must have unhooked the screen," he said, "shoved the bottom out and tossed the bottle."

Fred pushed the screen out farther until he had a clear view of the ground below. "It would have landed close to the front steps, easy enough for someone to pick it up in the morning, quickly throw it in the garage, and get back to where the others were waiting, probably without being missed."

"And the person may not have even thought anymore about it," Allison said, "until she, or he, saw Becky heading into the garage. Then it became vitally important that Becky not show it around." She gave Fred a satisfied smile. "It's all beginning to make more sense. Now where do we go from here?"

"I'll call in and get the fingerprint team back out here to do the window and screen. I doubt they got it earlier since the window wasn't open." Fred scowled. "But it really won't prove anything. Any member of the family could say they had opened or shut the window for Bess at some point. So I guess the next thing is to gather the clan again. Gail has already had them sign separate statements, but I'd like to talk to them again en masse. And so you, Ma'am, could find Gail and ask her to round up everybody in the library."

"Yessir, Boss, and just when do I get on the payroll?"

"If you solve this case, I'll put your name in for the reward."

"And what reward would that be?"

"Dinner with me at Cassie's Seafood Restaurant. They serve the best fried catfish and biggest hush puppies in the county."

"How could I turn that down?"

ALLISON HEARD LILLIAN and Gail talking as she neared the kitchen door. "I know I really have no business here anymore," Lillian said, "but I couldn't bear the thought of poor Teddy heading back to Charlotte on an empty stomach. He's such a sweet child. He told me that the cousins had agreed to give me my severance pay as soon as things are settled."

"I'm sure they're all very fond of you and appreciate the way you cared for their aunt," Gail said. "By the way, Teddy mentioned that the night of the murder he came down to the kitchen and finished the banana pudding." Gail paused. "He must have quite an appetite."

Allison waited in the hallway to hear Lillian's reply. "You're right about that. He's always hungry. Not only did he clean up the pudding, but also stuffed himself with several chocolate chip cookies. When I came in the next day, I saw the pudding dish in the sink and the cookie jar near 'bout empty. Just goes to prove what I told Catherine about that wife of his."

Gail took the bait. "And what was it you said about his wife?"

"That all she cares about is her acting and her jewelry. She's always showing off her fancy earrings and the bracelets she designs. She even brags that they let her into where they make the jewelry and if she wanted to, she could pick up some pure gold and stick it in her pocket. But she doesn't give a lick about cooking, doesn't care if Teddy gets a square meal or not. I don't know why he's so crazy about her. I just don't understand some men."

Allison came into the room, commented on the delicious smell, pulled Gail aside, and gave her Fred's message. As Gail and Allison left the kitchen, Lillian called after them. "Tell them it's potluck today. Anybody who wants can fix a plate. Oh, and tell Teddy I made some corn fritters just for him."

It didn't seem like a happy group that gathered in the library. Fred assured them his questions would only take a few minutes. They were each to leave information where they could be reached if needed for further questioning.

Paul came up to Fred. "I'm supposed to be back for services tomorrow. Do you need me for anything else?" Fred shook his head and waved him away. Catherine sat quietly in the corner. She glanced up at Paul and gave him a timid wave.

Allison walked out with Paul to the hallway. "How's Cat doing? She was pretty upset this morning."

"Better. We've talked. But you can't cover years of hurt and bitterness in a few minutes. I told her I'd like to keep in touch."

"And she agreed?"

"Well, she didn't disagree. I'm going to let things settle a little and then I'll visit if she'll let me. I'm only a couple of hours away. In the meantime, you'll be there to help her."

"I don't know that I'll be much help. I feel responsible for dredging up the past."

Paul shrugged. "Might have been for the best. I really think Catherine's relieved to have it out in the open. She told her cousins all about it when they came back a while ago, and they've rallied around her. She'll be all right."

FRED TOOK A MINUTE to focus on each one of the suspects as they gathered in the library. Catherine sat staring out the window, her eyes rubbed red, her hair pulled back with a rubber band, her tee shirt damp and rumpled, looking years older than she had only a few days earlier. He smiled approval as Allison pulled a chair up to her friend and gave her a brief hug.

In his mind Allison had never been a suspect, and her presence here had almost made the investigation enjoyable. It wasn't often he could talk business with a bright and personable woman. He couldn't say she was pretty, but her face showed character and caring and strength.

Derita sat on the other side of Catherine. Fred hadn't quite been able to figure her out yet. She seemed genuinely fond of her cousins and Charles's children. She was beautiful, her dress and makeup always perfect, her emotions under control. Maybe she was just a little too perfect. And where was she between the hospital and the motel last night?

Imogene stood out as another beauty, Fred thought, flawlessly and meticulously put together. He didn't know much about women's clothes or fashion, but he was sure she shopped only in the best stores.

His gaze went to the two brothers. Charles was the handsome one with a smile that would charm a snake. He had appeared to be cooperative, but there were still some loopholes in his story.

Teddy had taken advantage of Lillian's offering and came in from the kitchen bearing a plate loaded to the rim. His short frame was beginning to show the results of his hearty appetite: a developing paunch, belt fastened on the last notch, cheeks bulging out even when he was not smiling. He was not smiling now. "Let's get this show on the road. I've got a business to run."

"All right," Fred said. "We'll start with your business. What sort of deal had you made with Finnigan's Development?"

Teddy's fork stopped midway to his mouth. A hunk of ham slid off and plopped on the floor. Without hesitation, Imogene grabbed a piece of paper from the desk, knelt down, retrieved the meat, wiped the floor of any stain and tossed the paper into the waste basket. Fred observed all this with the thought, *Teddy's careless, and Imogene is accustomed to cleaning up after him.*

"So you know about that?" Teddy said, again turning his attention to his plate.

"I know you'd started surveying the woods, apparently without your aunt's permission. Suppose you explain that to us."

Charles stood up and approached his brother. "Yes, Teddy, suppose you do explain that. You were sneaking behind our backs to get what you wanted? Of all the low-down, contemptible, dirty…" Charles threw his hands in the air to finish the sentence. He paced the floor twice—to the window, back to Teddy—to the window, back to Teddy. Silence smothered the room. Fred decided not to say a word as he and the others watched the drama unfold. Fred knew Charles to be a reasonable man but also a man who was given to sudden outbursts of emotion. The detective wondered which aspect of his personality would prevail now.

On his third trip, Charles stopped and faced Teddy. He slowly unclenched his hands and took a deep breath. "Teddy, I know your business isn't going well. I know you need the money you'd get from developing the land with condos and whatever." He pulled up a chair, and put his hand on Teddy's shoulder. Fred sensed this was big brother talking to little brother whom he loved, the brother who had shared summer joys at the lake, the brother Charles was not going to forsake. "I want to understand, Teddy. But please tell me you weren't the one who hurt Aunt Bess or my Becky."

"No, Charles, I swear. I wasn't the one. I would never hurt Becky. I love your kids. I always wanted some of my own, but it didn't happen." Imogene stirred slightly in her chair, but didn't say anything. Catherine and Allison were giving their full attention to Teddy while Derita was now the one who stared out the window to the empty tennis court and the lake beyond.

Teddy turned to Fred. "You're right. I tried to negotiate a deal with Finnigan without Aunt Bess knowing. Derita and I thought we could convince

Aunt Bess it was a good business deal if we had some figures to show her."

"Derita was in on it too?" Charles exploded. All eyes turned to Derita except Fred's. He took the opportunity to study the eyes of the others: Charles's were angry, Teddy's wary, Imogene's smoldering, Catherine's and Allison's surprised. Derita returned all their stares with seeming indifference.

"Derita can tell her story later. Go on," Fred said to Teddy. "What kind of deal?"

"Nothing could be finalized until Aunt Bess agreed, but I had to prove to Finnigan the condo idea was feasible. So I told him to do some surveying on how the streets could be laid out, the lake access, how we could bring in the utilities and so on. And then I remembered Derita's idea of turning the lodge into a health spa and it occurred to me that the plans would benefit each other. That's when I called Derita and she agreed. Imogene and I came up in April to try to convince Aunt Bess of what a good business deal this would be."

Charles started pacing again. "And just where was this deal going to leave Catherine and me? Out in the cold?" He stopped in front of Teddy's chair. "And where did it leave Aunt Bess? She wasn't dead yet, you know. Or did you strike up a deal on that too?"

"No, damn it! But she was sick. She needed to be in a nursing home, not living here alone in this ghost of a house. I tried to reason with her. I wanted her to sell the land for development, agree to lease the lodge to Derita, and split the estate at her death among the four of us—which is what she planned to do anyway."

Catherine rose and came over to stand next to Charles. "But why now? Why couldn't the development have waited until Aunt Bess passed away? And then we could have discussed it."

Charles answered before Teddy had a chance. "Because he was getting a big kickback from Finnigan. Isn't that right, Brother?"

"So what? You two would have gotten your money eventually. I needed mine now!"

"But Aunt Bess wouldn't go along with you," Catherine said, "and that's when you called Derita in. Since she was Bess's favorite, you thought she would succeed where you had failed."

Fred sat contentedly at one end of the coffee table while Gail frantically took notes at the other end. No need for me to ask questions, he thought, they're doing fine by themselves.

"Yes, I thought she might have some influence. But I wasn't relying on her. I called Aunt Bess later with some solid numbers, and she sounded impressed. She said she would consider it, and I went forward on the assumption that I could make the deal."

"You knew you had lost the deal, though," Charles continued, "when Aunt Bess told all of us she was going to sell out to loggers. Is that when you decided to kill her?"

"No! I told you I didn't do it. Sure, I was going to lose a lot of money. The fact is I would have lost my shirt while waiting for the inheritance. But I didn't kill her. When could I have done it? Imogene and I were together all evening." Imogene patted his hand and nodded.

Catherine shook her head. "No, you weren't. I know you went back down to the kitchen."

"So I went to the kitchen. That's nowhere near Bess's room."

"Wait a minute," Catherine said, rubbing a trembling hand over her forehead. "I saw a light in the billiard room that night when we were out on the boat. Did you happen to go in there also?"

"Yeah. So what if I did? I was just looking at the game collection. Uncle Henry has some beauts in there."

"You were probably appraising them to see if you could pick up a few more easy bucks." Charles didn't keep the anger out of his voice.

"Or," Catherine said, "he could have walked up the stairs in there and come out right at Aunt Bess's door."

"That's right," Charles jumped in. "You could have crept up the stairs and gone into Aunt Bess's room without anyone seeing you."

Fred had not mentioned to anybody Allison's theory of the spray bottle containing the poison being planted earlier and retrieved later. Better to let them go at each other with their accusations and excuses. However, Gail chose this particular time to inject her own information. Fred wanted to shut her up, but he was too far away to kick her under the table.

"According to my notes," she said, "Teddy was gone from the room from a little after nine until after nine-thirty. But Mrs. Lattimer was alive at nine-thirty because she spoke to Derita."

"See there, I couldn't have done it. You two will have to come up with a better story than that to convict me."

Charles slumped down in the chair next to Teddy. "I'm sorry, Teddy. I wasn't trying to convict you, but I sure want to get to the bottom of this thing."

Fred decided it was time to take back the interrogation. "I have just one question for you, Imogene. Were you aware of Teddy's negotiations with the developer?"

Imogene leaned closer to her husband, gave him an adoring smile and answered in a deep Joan Crawford voice, "Of course I knew. Teddy doesn't hide anything from me. And he wasn't hiding anything from Bess either. He told her exactly what he wanted to do." Fred could picture her on the stage: composed, commanding, her audience taking in every word. "Teddy had a brilliant plan," she went on. "It would have meant a great deal of money for both of them. But the old woman was too stubborn to admit it." Imogene's voice began to rise. "She accused Teddy of being like his father, of having no business sense. She said he was 'as stupid as a blind turkey.'" Now there were tears in her voice and in her eyes. Fred couldn't tell whether they were real or manufactured.

"That was during your visit in April?" Fred asked.

Imogene nodded. "But Teddy thought he could still change her mind?"

"Yes. In fact he thought she had changed her mind when he called her back, but I knew she was just leading him on."

"You knew?" queried Fred.

"Well," Imogene hesitated. "I didn't really know. But Bess Lattimer was a cruel person. She enjoyed hurting people. I felt she encouraged Teddy just so she could hurt him that much more. She did that to me once." Imogene looked around the room. She had everyone's attention. Allison suspected the actress was playing for their sympathy. "Two years ago Bess sent me a card on my birthday. I was so pleased because she had never sent me a card—or anything before. But on the back of the card she had paper-clipped a piece she cut out from the theater section of the Charlotte paper. It was a review in which a critic had called my performance in *A Butterfly World* more like a dinosaur than a butterfly. She had highlighted the word 'dinosaur.' It was her idea of a joke." Imogene's voice broke into a sob. This time there was no doubt it was real. "She was a nasty person."

Fred was at a loss about what to say to the broken actress, but Charles then butted in with his own story. "Imogene's right, you know. I hate to say it, but Aunt Bess could be sadistic. She did almost the same thing to me. She made me think she would consider giving part of her holdings as a nature preserve. Then she blind-sided me with her announcement about clear-cutting the land. She really did know how to hurt people."

"Which brings us to your threat," Fred said. "You were reported to have said something about stopping her."

Gail was flipping through her notes. "He said, 'I'll stop you someway, somehow.'"

"Just how did you intend to stop her, Charles?"

"I don't know. I was angry. I don't even remember what I said."

"Do you remember where you were when you weren't in your room at ten-thirty the night of the murder?"

Charles threw up his hands. "All right. I did have a plan. I knew it would have a slim chance of succeeding, but I had to try something." Charles paused. Fred waited. "After the family meeting I called a couple of friends, fellow members of the Planet Alliance Association. I wanted to talk to them about holding a demonstration against the logging company. I didn't want anybody to know so I asked them to park down the drive and walk up. We discussed how we might go about it. I knew I couldn't change Aunt Bess's mind, but we thought we might intimidate the logging company into withdrawing their offer to buy the land."

"Hey, great idea," Teddy beamed at his brother. "But when were you going to do it? Bess said she was going to sign the papers the next morning."

Again Fred let the conversation roll on its own. "We knew we didn't have much time," Charles said.

"These guys are experts, though, at staging demonstrations on short notice. They have a bunch of college kids always ready to march for a good cause. The plan was to alert the media and then have demonstrators picket the downtown offices of the logging company."

Catherine spoke up. "So that explains the voices Wesley heard outside his window. But Charles, did you really think it would work?"

"We figured it might stall them off for a while until we could come up with something else. Of course, when Aunt Bess was found dead, it changed the situation. So as soon as I got the chance, I called and canceled the whole thing."

"Her death was very convenient for you, wasn't it?" Fred asked.

Charles sighed. "Yes, it was convenient. But it wasn't necessary. I could have stopped her without killing her."

Fred had to admit to himself the statement was probably true. I'm still in the dark, he thought, and only one more cousin to hear from.

FOURTEEN

DERITA STIRRED, gave a half-smile to Fred and to each of her cousins. "My turn?" Each head bobbed in response. Fred was suddenly exhausted. He didn't really care to hear what the lovely Derita had to say. He knew her story would make her sound just as innocent as all the others. He needed to get away, to go fishing, to go golfing, to do anything to rid his thoughts of everyone in this room—except, he corrected himself, for Allison. Maybe he and Allison could slip away, take a long ride in the country, forget all about poisons and bashed heads. But not yet. Derita was staring at him. "So what do you want to know?"

Fred put his detective hat back on. "For starters, suppose you tell us where you went when you left the hospital last night."

"For a ride. I was going to look in on Mom and Dad, but decided it was too late. So I just drove around. I was too upset to sleep."

"Upset about what?"

"About everything: Aunt Bess, Becky, knowing we were all under suspicion, wondering who could have done such terrible things. I had to clear my head.

I drove for maybe an hour and then went to the motel."

Fred knew he had to ask and also knew what her answer would be. "Did you go out to the Blue Goose during your drive?"

"No. I drove north of town, by the golf course and the college."

"Stop anywhere?"

"No. Oh," Derita said, her smile getting larger, "I do remember passing a semitrailer. He honked his horn as I went by and I waved at him. I'm sure if you can find that trucker he'd remember me."

"Yes," Fred agreed. "I'm sure he would. Now back to Teddy and his plan. Did you talk to your aunt about it?"

"Sure did. I called and again she was very nice on the phone. Said she would think it over. I came here a couple of days earlier than the others to reinforce the idea. She never disagreed, except about the nursing home part. She said she would never go into a home, but said she didn't care what happened to the place after she was gone. She said it didn't matter to her if it were made into a fat farm, a shopping plaza or a kiddie jungle."

"Or clear-cut?" Charles added.

"She never mentioned that—or moving to Arizona. I thought she meant she didn't care what happened to the place after she died. As it turned out, she had no intention of dying."

"Until someone changed her mind," Fred said.

"Wasn't me. Sure, I hated to see the lodge destroyed and the trees cut, but the truth is, it just wasn't that important to me."

"I see. That didn't seem to be your fiancé's impression."

"You talked to Bruce?" For a moment Derita's face lost its mask of indifference.

"Let's say I made some inquiries. The information I received is that you promised Bruce you'd transform the lodge into a health spa according to his specifications. You even obtained the floor plans of the Blue Goose and gave them to an architect to plan the alterations needed. True?"

Derita didn't lower her gaze. "You've got it partially right. I did promise Bruce a spa. We're going to run it together. I wanted the lodge. The location is perfect. The ambiance is fantastic. But if I couldn't get it, I was prepared to buy some other property. Daddy was going to loan me whatever money I needed. I tell you the Blue Goose wasn't that important to me."

Fred ran his fingers through his hair. His head was beginning to feel like the inside of a drum at a football game. "I guess that about wraps it up. You can go now. I'll be in touch."

The cousins rose in relief and started for the door. Gail's voice stopped them. "May I ask one more question?" Her appeal was to Fred.

Fred tried to keep the irritation out of his voice. "Be my guest."

Gail flipped through her notebook. "Derita, I want to check the time again when you said you finished your shower and thought you heard a noise in your aunt's room."

"Like I said before, I don't know the exact time, but I think it was about nine-thirty. I asked her if she was all right and she answered me. Why do you ask?"

"I wondered if you could be mistaken. The coroner said she could have died as early as eight."

"Well, she didn't. I heard her and it was close to nine-thirty. Why would I make it up? If I'd wanted to kill her, I could have done it anytime. No one would have seen me enter her room. I could have said I heard her voice at midnight if I wanted to lie about it."

"But you didn't hear anything after you checked the window?"

"No. I was using my blow dryer, but I would have heard her if she'd cried out."

Gail seemed satisfied, but Fred asked to be sure, "Anything else?" Gail shook her head and the cousins deserted the room.

"I'd better go pack," Allison said to Fred. "Catherine's probably as anxious to get gone as the others are."

"Do you think she'd mind going home alone? I could drive you later. I owe you a dinner for all your help."

"But I didn't solve the crime." Allison's voice faltered. "I was so sure we'd come up with the answer. Now they'll be gone and we've got exactly nothing."

"Are you a good cook, Allison?"

The question surprised her. "Not particularly. And what has that to do with anything?"

"Well, I am. I can make a perfect beef stew, a pot of butter beans to swoon over and chili hot enough to keep you warm all winter. Know the secret?"

"Apparently not, since no one has ever swooned over my cooking."

"Simmering. That's the secret. You have to simmer the dishes for hours, on the back burner, on low heat. You can't hurry them."

"So?"

"So the same principle applies to solving a puzzle or a mystery or a crime. It's got to simmer in our brains."

Allison nodded. "On the back burner. On low heat."

"You got it. In the meantime, we put our minds on something else. We take a long relaxing drive, talk about the weather, swap recipes, tell each other a few lies, and then go our separate ways. Then one day, the pot will begin to boil over and…."

Allison started laughing and finished the allegory, "And spill the beans!"

CATHERINE HAD no objection to driving home alone. "I need some time to sort things out: all that's happened, where I go from here."

The two women embraced. "I'm sorry I wasn't here for you more, Cat. I guess I got too caught up in playing detective."

Catherine gave a knowing grin. "Or did you get too caught up *with* a certain detective?" Allison felt herself blushing. "He's a nice guy, Allison," Catherine said. "Maybe this won't be the last case you two work on together."

Allison pretended not to hear Catherine's last remark. "Are you sure you don't mind going back alone?" she asked.

"Not at all. I'll call you in a couple of days and we'll do lunch. And Allison, thanks for being a friend."

"Sure." Allison wheeled around and headed for the front porch. She decided she needed one more look at the lake before leaving. She wanted to remember it as a place of beauty, not as the enemy who had tried to take her life. As she meandered down the hill, Allison spotted Jake rowing toward the dock. She sat in a yard chair by the shore and waved at him.

The old man crawled out of the boat, carefully secured it and hobbled over to her. "Moving kind of sluggish today. Humidity, you know. But I had to come over to say good-bye to the younguns. They're good kids. And there were times when Bess didn't do them right, especially Catherine. You know what I mean?"

"Not really," Allison said. "Tell me about it."

Jake rubbed the gray bristle on his chin and looked up toward the lodge and then back at Allison. "I reckon you really ought to know the whole truth. Let me see them off and I'll be back."

"I'll be here." Allison waited impatiently. What more could Jake add to Catherine's horror story? She soon found out.

Jake began. "I talked to Paul before he left. He told me of Catherine's revelation. He's very concerned about her. Paul's a fine fellow. If things were different, their friendship might have a chance to develop into something more. But Bess made sure nothing like that would ever happen for Catherine."

"I don't understand."

"She told Catherine how much her father had suffered seeing his wife's illness progress. And Bess made Catherine swear she'd never inflict that kind of pain on another man and that she'd never pass the curse on to a child of her own."

"That explains why my matchmaking efforts never made it to first base. But how do you know all this?"

"Catherine came to me that day after Bess had told her about her mother and the accident. I guess I was like a surrogate uncle to her, and she needed someone to talk to." Jake's lonely eyes gazed across the still water and Allison wondered if that was the end of his tale. It wasn't. Jake took a deep breath. "But Bess had left something out, and I felt it was my duty to tell Catherine the rest. I still wonder if I should have."

"What rest?"

"Bess was urging her brother to put Adele, his wife, in a nursing home and then get a divorce. Bess was going to pay for everything. She said he should make a life for himself—and not be dragged down by some crazy woman. But Adele suspected what was going on, and I guess she couldn't face it. You know what happened next."

"Yes. Adele drove into the river and took her family with her."

Jake closed his eyes and shook his head. "It was Bess's fault. I've tried to believe Bess was doing what she thought best, but the fact is she was responsible for the tragedy."

"And you told Catherine that?"

Jake bowed his head. Allison barely heard his whispered, "Yes."

Allison closed her eyes and shook her head, "No wonder Catherine hated her aunt."

FIFTEEN

ALLISON KNEW FRED would be ready to leave soon, and she still had to finish packing. She also felt like she needed a change of clothes. Up until now Fred had only seen her dressed in jeans and sloppy tee shirts. If they did stop for dinner someplace, she wanted to look halfway decent. She pulled out a pair of dress slacks and a peach-colored blouse. She started to brush back her no-nonsense hair like she always did for gym class, glanced into the mirror, and changed her mind. Instead, she tried teasing the top just enough to give it some height and a semblance of bangs and a little width over her ears. It seemed to soften her face and made her feel more feminine. Satisfied it was the best she could do for now, she grabbed her bags.

Allison took a last look out her bedroom window to what Derita had called "the forest of the night creatures." It hadn't been just a childhood fancy. Some evil creature, bringing death in its wake, had indeed crept into this house during the night. Now everyone was leaving and the creature was still loose.

Fred was on the phone when Allison came downstairs. She sat on the back steps, stroking Lancelot and waving good-bye to each car as it left the drive, muttering to herself, "Is he the one? Is she the one?" As the dust settled, she looked deep into the cat's lemon-colored eyes. "You probably saw the whole thing. Which one was it? Who hid the spray bottle? Who is our basher?"

Lillian came out to empty the trash. "You taking that cat with you?"

"Me? I haven't thought about it. Aren't you going to take care of him?"

"Not me. I can't stand a cat, especially one who keeps sneaking into the house. Charles told me to clean up the lodge and keep an eye on it until things were settled, but he never said anything about the cat."

Lancelot rubbed against Allison's legs and started purring as if his life depended on it. Allison was conquered. "Could you feed him for a few days while I check with the others? If no one else wants him, I'll come back and pick him up." Lancelot must have understood. He pounced up in Allison's lap and gave her a thank-you lick on the cheek.

FRED SLAMMED OUT the door. "They found it! The spray bottle! In the hospital trash just like you said." Allison jumped up spilling Lancelot on the ground. Fred gave her a quick hug. "You're quite a detective, Ma'am. I may have to put you on the payroll after all."

"Any fingerprints?"

"They should know by the time we get to the office. You ready?"

Allison said good-bye to Lillian, promising to call in a few days regarding the cat. Fred loaded Allison's bags in the trunk and Allison started to climb into the back seat. Fred shook his head. "You ride up front with Gail. It's not often I can relax in the back seat."

"Don't believe him," Gail said, as she carefully slid her notebook between the front seats. "He rides in the back every chance he gets. Closes his eyes and claims to be thinking."

"I close my eyes so her driving doesn't scare me to death. Gail hasn't admitted it yet, Allison, but I think she was on the NASCAR circuit before joining the department." Fred stretched his legs across the seat with a tiny bit of space to spare. It was one advantage to being short, along with not being expected to run fast, and always being in the front row of group photos. "We'll check in at the office, get the fingerprint reports on both the bottle and the pipe, then get my car and take off."

Gail tore out of the drive, at the same time looking back at her superior officer. "That's mighty considerate of you."

"What is?" Fred asked even as he shut his eyes. He had no real interest in Gail's answer.

"It's considerate of you not to use the police car to take Allison out on your first date."

Fred didn't move, his only reaction was a slight upward turn to his lips and a very low "Uh-huh."

THE FINGERPRINT REPORTS were disappointing, but not surprising. Prints on the spray bottle had been wiped clean, while those on the piece of metal pipe had been blurred by the water and sand. An exciting discovery occurred about the pipe, however. The hair and blood, embedded in the grooves, matched Becky's. Although there was no hair on it matching Allison's, Fred concluded the same weapon had been used on both victims. "The assailant couldn't have run to the lake and hidden the pipe under the pier after hitting Becky without being seen. It had to have been hidden somewhere near the garage or house and then retrieved when needed again."

The other report of the spray bottle was even more exciting. Allison squealed in delight when she finished reading it, "This proves it was the murder weapon." Fred had already read the report, but listened patiently while Allison read parts of it aloud. "Traces of sodium cyanide found in the nozzle of the bottle and sulfuric acid in the base." She turned to Fred. "What was the sulfuric acid for?"

"It turned the cyanide powder into a poisonous gas. Instead of putting the cyanide into her food which would have been quite obvious, the killer tired to make it look like a natural death by letting her inhale the gas, killing herself as you've already suggested." Fred reached for a dusty book on a shelf behind his desk. After reading a minute, he informed Allison. "The gas is called hydrocyanic acid. It's used in some states to execute criminals."

"Oh, my gosh," Allison gasped. "Do you think it was meant to be symbolic? That is, the murderer considered Bess Lattimer a criminal for what she was doing to the land and that this was a deserved execution?"

Fred shook his head. "Possible, of course. But I think when we get to the bottom of this mess, all we're going to find is someone with plain old-fashioned greed."

"And someone with the knowledge of how to make a poison gas. It's not something I learned in Chemistry 101."

"Maybe you were absent that day. The information isn't hard to come by. But our criminal was quite clever in going about it. You see, the two ingredients couldn't be combined ahead of time. It had to be done just before the gas was needed for its victim. The murderer arranged it so Bess would do the combining herself to produce the poison gas."

"How on earth was that done?"

"Notice the report states the cyanide was found in the nozzle while the acid was in the base. To activate the nasal spray, the nozzle has to be pushed down and then released. That's when the patient inhales to get a breath of the spray. So when Bess depressed the nozzle, the cyanide was dropped into the acid and *voila!* Poison gas appears as if my magic."

Allison nodded her head in admiration. "Our murderer is no dimwit."

"Unfortunately," Fred said, "none of the suspects are dimwits, so our search isn't narrowed one tiny bit. What we need to concentrate on now is where the ingredients came from. Sulfuric acid would be no problem, but finding pure sodium cyanide would be a little tricky." Fred twirled his desk chair around and motioned to Allison. "Sit down and make like a whirligig. Maybe you'll come up with the answer."

Allison sat. She twisted. She swivelled. She spun around. "All I'm coming up with is sea sickness and more questions. Are you saying this cyanide is not the kind one might find in something like rat poison or whatever?"

"It's used in certain industries, but a person doesn't walk into a drug store and take it off the shelf."

"Could one ask the druggist for a wee bit of cyanide to kill some pesky neighborhood dogs?"

"Not a chance." Fred frowned. "And I'm appalled you would say something like that. I thought you were an animal lover."

"Well, I am, but I prefer cats to dogs."

Gail peeked back into the office. "I thought you two were on your way out of the county."

"We are," Fred said. "We're going to forget all about murder and poison and clues and suspects. We're going to enjoy a lovely June evening, drive with the windows open, stop at some dimly lit restaurant, and gorge ourselves on steak and shrimp."

It was a quiet drive. Fred slipped in a John Denver tape and they didn't talk much. The silence was comfortable, the music soothing, and the wind smelled of honeysuckle. It was only after they pulled into the parking lot at Berdini's Fine Dining that Fred felt compelled to say something. "Never been here, but I've heard good things about it. Look tolerable to you?"

"I don't know. There seems to be a dearth of pick-up trucks and motorcycles and I don't see a flashing Budweiser sign but," Allison grinned, "they might make a decent burger here."

The building was low, painted a subdued cypress green with shutters a shade darker. Mock-orange bushes flanked the entrance, their creamy white blossoms reflecting the retreating sun. Inside, the late afternoon heat and light was banned by tilted blinds; lazy fans circled overhead and above the bar hung a picture of Capri, its hillsides draped with bougainvillea. "Nice," Allison whispered. "Does it come equipped with singing waiters?"

"If it doesn't, I'll do the honors myself. I'm sure you've heard of Freddie Lanza, the singing detective."

Allison rewarded him with a belly laugh. "Of course, and he has a partner known as Raggedy Allison, the dancing gym teacher turned super sleuth."

It was good to have someone to laugh with, Fred thought. He suddenly realized how seldom he did laugh. It wasn't something he grew up with. The only child of a stern father and a humorless mother, he'd often heard, "I don't see anything funny about that," when he'd tried to tell them of a comical happening or to repeat a schoolyard joke. In college he had to study too hard to have much time for foolishness. And there certainly wasn't anything funny about his present job. It seemed his entire life had been somber and sober.

He began to feel just a little giddy and decided to try out a joke he'd heard that morning on the radio. "Did you hear the one about the goldfish who said to his companion in the fishbowl, 'I feel like I've been going around in circles all day.'?"

Instead of a laugh, Allison gave him a pity-smile. "If that's the best you can do, we'd better order. Your brain needs a little nourishment."

During dinner, the conversation became a little more serious. "Tell me about those two college kids of yours," Fred said.

Allison beamed. "Sure. I love to talk about my kids. Connie and Dave. They're sweet. Although there was a time a few years ago when I called them Bonnie and Clyde. Thank goodness, they grew out of that stage." Allison put her fork down, cupped her chin in her hand and got a faraway look in her misty brown eyes. "I miss them, miss them being underfoot, miss their constant little bickering, miss their voracious appetites, their unanswerable questions." She took a sip of coffee and smiled at Fred. "I guess what I miss most is the sense of being needed. You know, a person needs to be needed."

Fred cleared his throat. He didn't quite understand what she meant and didn't want to ask. So he asked instead, "What are they studying?"

Allison's eyes lit up, and Fred could see pride taking the place of the earlier loneliness. "Connie's in premed. She has one more year before med school. Wants to be a pediatrician. Dave's more like me, plans to be a teacher. He's not really sure what field yet. This is his first year, so he has plenty of time to decide. They're both doing great."

"Of course they are. They have a great mother."

Even in the dim light, Fred could see the color rise in Allison's face. She seemed to be concentrating on buttering an onion roll and didn't answer. He wondered if he had overstepped some invisible boundary.

When she did answer, it was preceded by a little sigh. "It's funny how roles are reversed as time goes by. Now they worry about me."

"What's to worry about?"

"Me being alone and all that stuff."

Fred nodded. "I know about being alone—and all that stuff. But I don't have anyone to worry about me." He bowed his head for a moment and then came up with a worried frown. "Of course, I don't go around getting myself bashed in the head either. Your kids have a right to worry about you. Are you going to tell them about your murder weekend?"

"Only the highlights. I'll kind of skim over my misadventure on the pier."

"Speaking of which…" Fred's voice trailed off as he chomped the last of his steak. "What was it you were telling me about writing poetry while you sat there?"

Allison laughed. "Well, I wasn't actually writing, you know, just composing in my head. Lines of poetry pop into my mind at the weirdest of times. It's a malady I've suffered since childhood. My mother accused me of always day-dreaming, but that wasn't the case. It's just when I see something or hear something so beautiful that it seems beyond description, I want to capture it, make the scene live forever."

"So what was so beautiful that night? The moonlight on the water?"

"No. The moon hadn't come out yet. Actually my poem was about the sounds."

"But you said you didn't hear anything—no one creeping up on you."

"I guess the reason I didn't hear anybody was because of the other sounds."

"What other sounds? At night the lake is as quiet as a morgue."

"Oh, no. At night there's a whole orchestra playing by the water's edge." Allison took a deep breath. "Do you want to hear my poem?"

Fred sensed this was a special moment, and he didn't want to mess it up. "Sure," he whispered. "I'd like that."

Allison put her fork on the table, laced her fingers and swallowed hard.

Summer stereo
Crickets chirruping shrilly
Bullfrogs bassooning.

Fred waited for her to go on. She didn't. Instead Allison gave an embarrassed giggle. "That's all. That's the poem. It's called haiku."

The detective shook his head as if he was missing some clues. "Hi-what?"

"Haiku. It's a form of Japanese poetry. It tells something about nature and seasons, using only seventeen syllables." Allison shrugged her shoulders. "I know it doesn't sound like much, but I enjoy the form. It's a mental challenge." She laughed. "You should try it some time."

"I have enough mental challenge trying to solve crimes, thank you very much. I think I'll leave the poetry writing to you." Fred lined up his knife and fork on the edge of his plate. "Is all your poetry that lofty?"

"No. Some of it is downright trite."

"Give me an example."

"Here's a limerick I wrote during the last election. Try not to laugh.

There once was a candidate called Billy
Who made promises willy-nilly
At a county fair booth
He choked on the truth
And that was the end of poor Willy.

Fred grinned. "That's more to my liking."

"Then maybe you'll like my parodies."

"What's a parody?"

Allison sipped her coffee and pondered a minute. "I guess you could call it a take-off on something already written."

"Can you give me an example?"

"For instance, take the children's song 'Go Tell Aunt Rhody.' It goes in part like this:

Go tell Aunt Rhody
The old gray goose is dead.
The one she's been saving
To make a feather bed.

Now my parody would go something like:

Go tell the cousins
The old Blue Goose is dead.
The one they were hoping
Would feather all their beds.
Go tell the cousins
The Blue Goose is dead.

Fred shook his head and rolled his eyes. "There's just no end to your talent." "It's something to do during long, lonely evenings. "I think I could come up with something better than that." "Really? I'm open to suggestions." Fred was glad for the dim lighting as he felt his face getting red. "We'll go into that later. Right now, we have the mental challenge of deciding on dessert."

"That's no problem. Just order me anything that's decadently chocolate."

IT WAS LATE when they reached Allison's home. A streetlight illuminated the one story brick house that was nearly identical with its neighbors on either side. The house was surrounded by azaleas, and the smallish front yard displayed a lone cedar tree with a tiny bluebird house.

Allison dug in her purse and brought out her house key. "You need to come in and have a cup of coffee before starting back. You look like something washed up on the beach after a storm."

"I feel worse than that. Do you think the neighbors would talk if I didn't go back home tonight?"

"Of course they would. My neighbors are as nosy as I am. I can warrant you that both Clarisse, to my south, and Malvina, on my north side, heard your car drive up and are at this very moment peeping through curtains to see who has brought me home at this ungodly hour." Allison opened the door wide, flipped on the hall light and ushered Fred in. "Might as well give them a good look. But the fact that Clarisse is a member of the school board and that the board takes a dim view of questionable behavior by their teachers and that my very livelihood depends on the school board liking me, I doubt if allowing you to spend the night would be a reasonable exercise in good judgement."

Fred yawned. "For a school teacher you surely do ramble on. I think you need a refresher course in concise sentences."

"And you need some New Orleans style coffee, guaranteed to keep your eyes open for at least four hours."

"I can make it home in about two hours. What do I do the rest of the time?"

Allison busied herself with the coffee maker. You can think about me, she mused, because I'll be thinking about you: about your kindness, about your smile, about how I'd like to get to know you better. Aloud she said, "Play solitaire."

The next day Allison called Connie and then Dave. She caught up on their doings, pretended interest in Connie's biology lab and Dave's latest girl. They fleshed out their earlier plan for the family to spend a week together at Atlantic Beach in August. And then they finally got around to asking, "And how was your lake vacation, Mom?"

"Oh, it was all right. Didn't get in much swimming, however, because of the murder."

SIXTEEN

ALLISON WAITED a couple of days and then called Catherine. "How about lunch at the Westend Grille?" Allison had really wanted to invite Catherine to her house, but remembered Fred's instructions for her not to be alone with any of the suspects. Although she'd never really considered Catherine a suspect, Allison didn't want to go against Fred's advice.

"Well, I don't know," Catherine said. "I don't much feel like going out or talking."

"Oh, do come. We'll have iced tea and warm conversation. And if you wish, we'll confine the conversation to the weather and baseball."

SETTLED IN A SMALL BOOTH, iced tea in their hands and Philly steaks on the way, they agreed the weather was tolerable and the Braves were off to a good start. Allison thought now might be a good time to bring up the disposition of Lancelot. "I'd love to have the cat, but I need to be sure neither you nor any of your cousins want him."

Catherine gave her tea a quick stir. "Pets aren't allowed in my apartment complex, which is fine with me since I'm not particularly fond of cats anyway. If you like I can call each of the others and ask them."

"Please do and let me know. I'll run down Thursday morning to pick up the cat if it's all right with everybody."

"Sure. I'll call them tonight."

There was a long pause. Finally Allison said, "Fred told me not to think about the murder for a few days, to let it simmer. But it's hard. Not to think about it, I mean."

"I know. It keeps going around and around in my head." Catherine gave a half-smile. "It reminds me of the tornado scene from *The Wizard of Oz* with furniture and everything flying in circles. That's the way my thoughts are: Aunt Bess, the cousins, Paul, what I'm going to do now that my secret is out."

Allison reached out and touched Catherine's hand which had begun to tremble, clanging ice against the side of her glass. "I'm so sorry," Allison said. "It's my fault. I shouldn't have questioned you about your disease."

"It's all right." Catherine sat her tea down and massaged her hands. "Actually it's rather a relief not to try to hide it any longer. But I'm worried about my job. I'm going to tell the superintendent, but maybe he won't want me to teach. Maybe the school board will think my problem will disturb the students. Actually I can control my trembling pretty well when I'm sitting behind the desk. It's when I have to get up to the blackboard that bothers me."

"Don't worry. The Disabilities Act should protect you. As long as you can do your job, they can't terminate you. And they have to make reasonable accommodations. Things will work out." Allison hesitated. "I admit I don't know much about Huntington's. Isn't there some treatment?"

"There are medications that help control symptoms, which I'm already taking. And of course, there's research and experiments. The trials of fetal tissue transplants appear hopeful. I'm sure there'll be a cure in the future. I just don't think it will happen in time to help me." Catherine looked up as the waitress brought their order. She took a big bite of the sandwich and said between chews, "Fortunately, it hasn't affected my appetite."

Allison waited while the waitress refilled their glasses and wondered what to say next. She wanted to encourage her friend without using trite or untrue aphorisms. Catherine's next statement solved Allison's dilemma. "Paul has helped me a lot. He's so understanding, so perceptive. It's like having a big brother saying, 'I know how you feel, Sis.'"

"So Paul has called you?"

"Several times. I know he's a preacher, but he doesn't talk like a preacher. He talks like he's a friend and he tells me that God is my friend also. I'm beginning to believe him."

CATHERINE CALLED later that night to report on her conversations with the cousins. "Lancelot is yours, Allison. In fact, everyone is very pleased that you're willing to take him. It's the only thing we've agreed on in a long time."

"Great. I'll run out tomorrow and buy a kitty carrier."

"No need to. Teddy reminded me there's one in the basement. It's one Aunt Bess used to carry the first Lancelot to the vet. Also, Charles said that Lillian found the keys to the house, so it's locked up now. I called Lillian and she said she would place the key under a brick behind the garbage can. You can let yourself in to get the carrier and then lock up afterwards."

"Will do. I'm looking forward to having a little company around this lonesome house, even if it is only a four-legged creature."

ALLISON WONDERED if she should call Fred and tell him she was coming down but decided against it. Instead, she'd pop in and surprise him. Maybe he'd even go with her to the lodge and then they could have lunch together. But the closer she got, the more nervous she became. *Will he think I'm using the cat as an excuse to see him? Did I read more into our dinner together than he intended?* Shyness overtook her, and she drove on past the station without stopping.

As Allison turned into the narrow, rutted driveway, then down the hill and beyond the loblolly pines, she remembered her first view of the lodge. Then, it had seemed spooky. Now it appeared downright phantasmal. She halfway expected poor Bess's ghost to peer out at her from behind closed drapes, complaining it couldn't rest until her murderer was found and brought to justice. "I'm doing my best," she explained out loud to the car steering wheel. "I just can't get all the clues to fall into place. Maybe by coming back to the scene of the crime, I'll shake loose some cosmic dust." The more she thought about it, though, the more nervous Allison became about being back at the Blue Goose, all alone— except for Bess's mournful spirit. "Lancelot, you'd better appreciate what I'm going through for you."

As she stepped out of her car, Allison spotted the orange puff of fur curled up on the back step, snoozing away without a care in the world. At the sound of his name, the cat lifted first his ears and then his head, surveyed his visitor and apparently decided he might be able to purr a few choice bars for her. He stretched, ambled over to Allison, gave her left leg a light nuzzle, droned out a subtle purr, and then retreated just enough to judge her reaction. Allison understood Lancelot didn't want to put forth any more effort than was necessary to reach his goal. And his goal at this time seemed to be a tasty tidbit. Allison responded by digging into her pocket and coming out with a plastic bag of Kitty Kandy. She poured a few of the tiny morsels into her hand, offered them to Lancelot and he, in turn, accepted them graciously. "Now," she said, "you wait here while I find the carrier and we'll be on our way. This place is giving me the creeps."

Of course, Lancelot had no intention of waiting

there. As Allison located the key, unlocked the door and stepped into the lodge, Lancelot was right between her legs. When she flipped on the basement light located outside its door, he rubbed her ankle, and when she started down the flight of stairs, he scooted ahead of her.

At the bottom of the stairs, Allison gave a quick look around, thinking the cat carrier would be in plain sight. It wasn't. So she started again, this time looking more carefully. To her right was an enormous furnace. Catherine had told her the lodge had been heated by coal before her Uncle Henry got smart and converted to electric heat. To the side of the furnace was a small pile of coal, a monument to a long-ago era. Above the pile was a rectangular door about two by two feet. Allison recognized it as a coal chute. She remembered her grandparents' cellar in West Virginia with its huge furnace and the chute where coal poured from truck to bin to be ready for the coal shovel which fed the fiery furnace.

Her eyes going on around the room, she saw a step ladder, a push broom and finally, stuck in the corner, the carrier. She hauled it out, disturbing years of dust which triggered a sneezing fit. When she had her nose back in control, she headed for the stairs, Lancelot at her heels. She'd just reached the bottom step when the light went out. She stubbed her toe and let out a loud "Damn! A fine time for the bulb to burn out." She thought of her flashlight carefully tucked in the glove compartment of her car. "A fat lot of good that flashlight does me. It's never around when I need it.

"Well, come on, Lancelot. We can't stay here. We'll have to fumble our way up the stairs." Which is just what she proceeded to do. Allison hung onto the railing, took one cautious step at a time and dragged the carrier behind her. She had left the door open a crack so there was a sliver of light to guide her. She was nearly at the top when the light disappeared. She heard the door shut tightly followed by a slight scraping sound. At first she was annoyed with herself. She remembered leaving the back door open and thought that a breeze must have blown the cellar door shut.

She continued on up to the top step, found the doorknob in the darkness, turned it, and pushed. Nothing happened. She tried again. The door was not budging. She recalled seeing a sliding bolt above the knob on the outside. Allison realized now the scraping sound she'd heard must have been the bolt being shoved over.

Terror flooded over her. Someone had locked her in the cellar. She knew instantly who it was. It was the same person who had botched the first attempt on her life. Now the assailant had come back to finish the job!

SEVENTEEN

ALLISON ADDED to her previous thought as she muttered, "It's bound to be the same person who bashed my head, but who is that?" The list of suspects remained the same. She had very foolishly notified each one of them about her plans to return to the lodge to pick up the cat. And even more foolishly had not stopped to tell Fred. Now what? What would happen next? She tried to calm the panic that arose in her chest, to stifle the scream which tried to push its way out of her throat. Carefully, Allison worked her way back down the stairs, grasping the railing with one hand and still holding the carrier with the other. When her foot hit the cement floor, she shoved the carrier back out of the way. "Looks like we're not going to need that for a while, Lancelot." The cat answered her with a reassuring ankle massage.

Allison's eyes were adjusting to the darkness and she realized it wasn't total. There were cracks of light around the coal chute door. It wasn't enough light to illumine anything but enough to give her some hope. She sat on the bottom stair step, trying to organize her thoughts, plan her next move. I'm safe, she thought, as long as the enemy is up there and I'm down here, but I need a lock on this side of the door to maintain that status.

Lacking a lock, Allison did the next best thing. She hauled out the carrier, lugged it again to the top of the stairs, and positioned it on the second step. Hopefully, anybody coming down the stairs would not likely see it until it was too late, would trip over it and end up in a heap on the cellar floor. Allison was confident she could then deal with whoever it was.

Allison strained to detect any sound of movement from above. She heard what she thought might be furniture being skidded across the floor, and then she heard the slam of the back door. "I'm just going to be left here? That's it? Well, Lancelot, that's not so bad. Somebody will come looking for me sooner or later." She comforted herself with the thought of her kids trying to call her and getting the answering machine. Or maybe Fred would call—or Catherine. How many times would they call, she wondered, before figuring out that she was missing? Would it take a couple of days? Several days? A sob escaped her lips. She reached down, peeled Lancelot from around her legs and buried her face in his fur. "Buddy, you and I have a lot of praying to do." And pray she did: for herself, for a way of escape, to be able to see the sun again, to laugh with her children again, to share another cup of coffee with Fred—and remembering a long ago Sunday School lesson, she prayed for her enemy. "Whoever it is, God, needs your help also—help out of evil and darkness."

Allison stood up and fanned herself with the front of her tee shirt. The weather forecaster had predicted temperatures in the mid-eighties today. It was probably now close to noon and she could already feel the heat increasing. "I've got to get out of here before I have a heat stroke." She stared at the shafts of light sneaking in around the coal chute and recalled that her grandparents' chute had only been fastened from the outside by a simple hook. If she could get up there, surely it wouldn't take much to bang against the door to open it and then she'd be able to crawl out to safety. Remembering seeing a step ladder, she edged her way around the wall to find it. Her hands touched the side of the furnace; it was cool and damp. Funny, she thought, for the furnace to feel cold when she was starting to perspire.

Her mind flashed back to gym classes. She'd always told her girls, no matter what game they were playing, in order to win they had to go beyond perspiration to sweat. Allison hadn't reached the sweat stage yet, but she was getting close.

She found the ladder, dragged it over to the coal bin, and propped it against the furnace. Now she needed to find something to hit against the chute door. Her grandfather had kept a long poker, curved at one end, which he had used to stoke the fire when it became sluggish. Allison made her way back to where she had seen the coal shovel, felt along the wall behind it and her hands touched something hard and cold and slim. It had to be a poker. But still, it was going to be a daunting task to get the ladder to stand upright on the pile of coal in order to get at the chute. Maybe, she thought, she should try the poker on the upstairs door first. She might be able to force it open and escape that way.

Once more, Allison found the steps and gingerly made her way up, careful to slide the carrier out of the way. The heat intensified with each step that brought her closer to the top. "I think that forecaster was a little off in his prediction," she informed Lancelot, whom she was sure was interested. "It must be ninety in here already."

As she readied the poker to pry against the door, Allison groped for the door knob. She found it, but her fingers immediately recoiled from the heat of the metal knob. She reeled back, missed a step, and grabbed the railing to steady herself. The smell of gasoline and smoke seeped under the door. It took only a second for her brain to register the fact that she was now in big trouble. Her enemy had locked her in the cellar and set the house on fire. For a moment she forgot her "love your enemy" philosophy and regretted praying for the demonic fiend who was trying to kill her. "Just get me out of here, God," she prayed again, "and we'll discuss that other part later."

Allison knew now her only way out was the coal chute door, and it had to be quickly. She surmised it wouldn't take long for fire to destroy the old lodge and her with it. She tried to remember how much coal she'd seen in the pile before the light went out.

Maybe if I plop the ladder into the middle of the pile, it'll stay there long enough for me to climb out. She grasped the ladder in front of her and stepped into the coal pile. The chunks of coal slipped, slithered, and cascaded around her feet. The ladder slapped against the wall and Allison slapped against the ladder. Crooking her neck, she glared at the miniature door, not yet within climbing distance. Hoisting the ladder again, she repositioned it closer to the wall and this time it felt like maybe she could make it. She hooked the poker by its curved end over a high rung, reached down and picked up Lancelot who was still pressing against her legs, and started to climb. The climb didn't last long. The coal under the ladder slid forward. The ladder, the poker, the cat, and Allison slid backward. Allison climbed out from under the ladder, spit coal dust out of her mouth, wiped smoke from her eyes—and started to sweat.

FRED WAS FINISHING UP routine paper work when Gail knocked on his door, then walked in without waiting for an invitation. "Just heard on the scanner the Blue Goose lodge is on fire. Trucks headed out. Think we ought to go?"

Fred took a second to digest the news, then he nodded. "It might have some bearing on our case."

ALLISON DECIDED the only way she was going to get the ladder to stay in place was to shovel some coal out of the way. She grabbed the shovel and tried moving the coal to one side and then the other. As she moved each shovelful, she heard other chunks sliding in to take their place. She wondered if she was making any progress at all. The heat was becoming unbearable and she started having choking spells. Allison didn't know if her choking and coughing were from the coal dust she was stirring up, or from smoke invading the cellar from above. She tore off her tee shirt and tied it around her face, leaving space for her eyes, although they were of little use to her. She kept turning her eyes to the cracks of light above her head. It evoked what she thought was a Biblical verse, "Truly the light is sweet." Her thoughts and prayers had dwindled. She only held onto one goal: to reach that light.

Using all the strength she had left, Allison lifted the ladder again, placed its base on the remaining coal, jiggled and wiggled it until the ladder crept through the chunks and found the floor. She took a tentative step up the first rung. The ladder held firm.

Above her, the noise of the fire had changed from a sinister sizzling to ominous crashes of either furniture or walls. Allison anchored the poker to the top rung and called for Lancelot. There was no answering purr or furry rub. "Come on, Lancelot. We don't have any time to waste." Her eyes stung, her muscles cried out for relief and her throat seemed to be closing. "Lancelot," she pleaded, "please come. We've got to get out of here. Talk to me."

If Lancelot answered, it was drowned out by a crash from overhead. Allison scrambled up the ladder, snatched the poker and started pounding on the chute door. By now she was so weak, the pounding was barely a tapping motion and not producing any results. In desperation she dropped the poker, turned sideways on the ladder and used her left shoulder as a battering ram. She heard the wood splinter as searing pain stabbed her shoulder. But she couldn't stop now. Blocking the pain from her mind, she gave one more tremendous push. It worked! The door broke open and sweet glorious light poured in. Allison figured she had broken something in her shoulder along with the door, but it didn't matter. She was nearly free. She stared out at the cool, green grass, reached her right hand up and grasped the edge of the opening. That's when she heard a tiny, pitiful meow.

She glanced back into the cellar, to the dark room that someone had intended for her burial vault. She didn't want to go back. But she had to. With the added light, Allison could now see Lancelot. He was crouched under a furnace pipe, either wedged tightly, or too frightened to move. Allison climbed down the ladder, fell again on the loose coal, cried out in pain, and scooped up the cat in her right hand. Now she faced another problem. She was unable to use her left hand or arm due to the pain and with Lancelot in her right hand there was no way for her to grasp the ladder rungs. Whispering reassurances to the panicked cat, Allison draped him, the best she could, around her neck and instructed him to hang on. He did, digging his claws into her bare neck and shoulders.

THE SIRENS CAME as Allison tumbled out of the coal chute door. She lay on the grass, exhausted but exhilarated. She ripped her tee shirt away from her mouth and gulped gobs of fresh air. At the same time she was trying to loosen Lancelot's claw-hold on her neck, and was sobbing, "Thank you, God, thank you." Amidst shouts of the firemen and the hissing of water on flames, Allison heard Jake's tremulous voice calling for Lancelot. The cat heard him too, released his hold on Allison's neck, and ran to a voice he had known in happier times.

Jake and one of the firemen turned opposite corners at the same time, spotting her on the grass. The fireman lifted her gently and carried her to the shade of a giant pin oak tree. "You'll be safe here," he assured her. "Anybody else in there?" Allison shook her head.

Jake came up and sat down beside her. "I'll stay with her," he assured the fireman. After the fireman was convinced she didn't need immediate medical attention, he left her and hurried back to his job.

Jake cradled Lancelot in one hand and held out her discarded shirt in the other. "Would you like to put this back on?"

Allison looked down at her bra, black with coal dust like the rest of her body. "I don't think I can. There seems to be something wrong with my left arm. Just throw it over me for now." Allison winced as Jake tried to tuck the tee shirt around her shoulders.

"Sorry, I didn't mean to hurt you." The old man

stared at Allison with worried eyes. "What are you doing here anyway?"

"Came down to pick up the cat, but he seems to be pretty happy with you. Want to keep him?"

"Naw. He'd just be a constant reminder of Bess. I've got to stop thinking about her all the time. In fact, that's what I was doing when I saw the smoke. I always enjoyed taking a mess of bream over here and sharing them with Bess. Then I remembered Bess wasn't here anymore. You know fried fish weren't meant to be eaten alone. I can eat a hamburger by myself or scrambled eggs or even a chicken leg—but not fish. A platter of fish requires companionship and conversation." Allison nodded. She understood how bereft he felt.

"So you saw the fire and called it in?"

"Yeah. Probably the wiring. I told Bess months ago the place needed rewiring. Lillian kept complaining about the clothes dryer tripping its switch. But Bess said the wiring was in better shape than she was and she wasn't about to spend any money on it."

Allison shook her head, but she didn't want to go into her ordeal with Jake. Let him think what he wanted to. He'd find out the truth soon enough.

THE FIREMEN WERE getting things under control when Fred and Gail drove up. Fred surveyed the scene, saw the parked car. "Whose car?" he asked the fireman who was hosing down the garage to keep the flames from gaining a foothold there.

"Probably belongs to the lady."

"What lady?"

"The lady in the front yard. I guess she was in the house when the fire started, but managed to get out. We haven't had time to get her story yet. Jake's with her."

Fred looked surprised. "What's Jake doing here?"

"He called it in. Saw the smoke from his place. Good fellow, that Jake. I've known him all my life. He said he'd stay with the lady until we had a chance to talk to her."

Gail motioned to Fred, pointing to the front yard. "Sure, go ahead," he said. "Find out what you can. Must be Lillian came back for something. I'll be there in a minute." He turned back to the fireman. "Any chance of saving the lodge?"

"Good chance, the front part anyway."

"Any idea what started it?"

"Not yet."

Gail came running back around the corner and yelled for Fred to come. When he reached the front yard, he saw the lady under discussion propped against a tree, covered with soot. It was only when she spoke that he recognized her. "Howdy, Partner," Allison said. "Good to see you."

Fred dropped down beside her, took her hand, and whispered, "Allison. Oh, Allison."

EIGHTEEN

THE X-RAYS REVEALED no fractures. "By tomorrow that shoulder will be one gigantic bruise," the emergency room doctor told Allison. "You're going to need rest and pain medications for about twenty-four hours. And antibiotic ointment on those abrasions and scratches."

"What she needs first is a good bath," Gail added. "If we don't get some of that black off you, Allison, I'm going to have to start calling you 'sister.'"

Allison grinned. "That would be all right by me. I bet you'd make a great sister."

"Glad you think so because you're coming home with me right now. We'll get you cleaned up, into a pair of my pajamas, and into bed. Fred can finish his questions later. He's quizzed you enough for tonight."

Fred sat on a chair across the room from Allison's stretcher. He stared into space, his hands folded in front of him. Allison had never seen him look so strange—so fierce. When the doctor left the room, Fred came over to the stretcher. Allison reached out her hand. Fred ignored it. "Yes," he said, "I've learned quite enough for tonight." There was none of the tenderness in his voice that Allison had heard earlier. After she'd told him how she had come to be at the lodge, he had clammed up. Now he just stood there and glared at her and when he spoke, his voice was harsh and angry. "Allison, for a teacher, you can be pretty stupid. I told you never to be alone with any of the suspects and what do you do? You tell each one of them you're coming to the Blue Goose, that you'll be by yourself. That's like sending engraved invitations to your own funeral."

Allison gaped in disbelief at this man she had considered kind and gentle, this man who had become her friend. Now he was standing over her and calling her stupid. She fought back tears which threatened to erupt. She may be stupid, but she wasn't going to be a cry baby. She tried to say something—anything—to defend herself. She couldn't. He was right; she'd told herself the same thing when she'd been battling for her life. But it hurt too much to hear it from him. Allison bit her lip and turned her head away.

Gail stepped between them. "You, Sir," she said to her superior officer, "can be excused. Go start checking some alibis or something. I'm taking Allison home with me. You can come by tomorrow if you think you can behave yourself." She turned her back and Fred stomped away.

"He gets that way when he's scared," Gail explained to Allison. "And right now he's scared he almost lost you."

FRED CAME BY the next morning—humbly apologetic. "I don't know what came over me. I guess I thought it was my fault: that I hadn't explained how dangerous your situation was, that you were taking things too lightly—or something." His voice fell. "I just don't know."

Allison was sitting at Gail's kitchen table, on her third cup of coffee, in her borrowed pajamas and robe. Traces of coal dust were still embedded under her nails. Other than that, and some lobster-red scratches on her neck, Allison showed little sign of her near-death ordeal. Physical sign, that is. Emotionally, she felt like a basket case. Two attempts on her life had been too much. She hadn't had time to think about it when she was imprisoned in that horrible cellar; she'd been too determined to get out, but now the implications overwhelmed her. Evil surrounded her, she thought. Someone was determined to destroy her—perhaps more than one. Maybe all the cousins were an evil team, intent only on their own desires. Would she ever be able to trust anyone again?

And Fred? She'd come to like him so very much. She'd dared to think their friendship might become something more. She'd even shared her poetry with him, something she hadn't been able to do with anyone in many, many years. But he too, had turned on her. Now he was apologizing. Could she accept that and go on?

Gail poured Fred a cup of coffee and then, with some excuse about checking the clothes dryer, she left them alone.

"Before I accept your apology," Allison said, "I need to ask you one thing. And I want the truth."

"Sure. Anything."

"When you asked to drive me home the other day was it because didn't want me to be alone with Catherine?"

Fred added another teaspoonful of sugar to his coffee and stirred it vigorously before answering. "Well, yes, but…"

Allison pushed back her chair and stumbled from the table. Anger and disappointment engulfed her. Again the question came: could she ever trust anyone again?

Fred caught up with her before she was able to flee the room. He put a gentle hand on her arm. "Please, hear me out." He motioned her back to the table and she followed his hand. He pulled out her chair and then scooted his own close to hers. "It was more than that." His voice was subdued, his eyes gentle.

"Sure I wanted to protect you, but I also wanted to get to know you better. You're the first girl— woman—female—whatever." Fred grinned as he bumbled over her category and Allison giggled. "Let me try that again," he said, "and don't laugh. You're the first dame that I've been drawn to for a long, long time." He finished in a rush and let out a sigh of relief.

Allison smiled, reached out, and touched his arm. "And you're the first man to call me a 'dame' in a long, long time."

AFTERWARDS, ALLISON WONDERED what might have happened next if Gail hadn't chosen that particular moment to re-enter the scene. She deposited Allison's washed and dried clothes on the table. "You'll have to relegate these things for your gardening clothes. Coal stains just don't wash out." Without waiting for either of them to comment, Gail reached for her notebook. "Now let's get down to business. What have you been able to find out, Fred?"

Fred slid back into his detective mode without a hitch, and Allison resumed her role as his partner. "Not one of them has an alibi," he said, slathering grape jelly on a piece of toast. "Oh, they all have good stories, but so far we haven't found any proof that they were where they said they were at the time of the fire. The sheriff's department in each county is going to keep checking for me."

"What are their stories?" Gail asked, her pencil poised. She had already recorded every fact Allison could remember about her harrowing experience.

"Charles spent the day bird watching, or rather bird searching. He said Baltimore orioles were reported to be increasing along some of the river banks, and he was trying to confirm it."

Allison recalled seeing orioles years ago, when visiting her grandparents. She'd been fascinated by the male's orange and black costume, as if he was dressed for Halloween. "How many did he see?"

"None." Fred slurped his coffee and went on. "Teddy said he drove around the countryside looking for fallow farm lands which might be transformed into housing developments. He figured if a farmer wasn't using his land, he might be willing to sell at a bargain price. Teddy still has a fantasy about striking it rich in real estate."

Gail looked up from her writing. "But no one can verify this?"

"Right."

"What about Imogene?" Gail had her pen ready again.

"She was out window shopping. It seems there were a lot of 'Midsummer Sales' advertised. She says she did the rounds of all the stores, ended up buying a linen jacket. She showed the jacket to the officer."

Allison was trying to pay attention, but she had taken another pain pill, and it was beginning to give her that floating feeling. "Did she have a receipt?"

Fred nodded. "The officer said it was dated, but no time showed on it. Most store registers automatically record the time also, but some of the older ones don't. Imogene told him it was around lunch time."

"So," Gail said, "that brings us to Derita."

"Derita said she and Bruce, her fiancé, had an argument the night before. She felt she had to be alone to sort things out in her head. So she took off to the beach where she sat and watched the waves all day."

"I can understand that," Allison murmured. "She didn't talk to anybody, probably didn't eat lunch and by evening she decided she had to go back home and face the future."

Fred studied his friend. "You talk like you were there."

Allison closed her eyes and winced. "I've been there."

Fred cleared his throat. "And then there's Catherine." Allison jerked up; she was hoping Cat could be deleted from the list of suspects. Fred avoided looking at Allison as he went on, "Catherine said she was in her apartment all day, catching up on some reading. The apartment manager can't say if she was or wasn't. The apartment building has a large parking lot in back. Cars come and go; no one pays any attention."

Gail closed her notebook. "So up to this point, we haven't eliminated a single suspect."

THAT AFTERNOON Allison convinced Gail and Fred she was fit to travel: the pain had become tolerable, she could move her arm enough to drive, and she was anxious to get home. Fred went to the hardware store, bought a new cat carrier, and fetched Lancelot from Jake's. "Call me as soon as you get home," he commanded her. "And then just take it easy. The pot's still simmering. You can't hurry these things. The answer will come in its own time." He opened the door for her, stood back while she got in, then bent down, and kissed her on the cheek. "And be careful," he whispered.

"Think the culprit will try again?"

"Not likely. All the suspects know we're watching them. But be careful—Partner."

FRED CALLED ALLISON the following afternoon. After she reassured him regarding her health, he asked, "Is the pot beginning to boil yet?"

"No. Still just simmering. I think we need to add some more ingredients. Anything new?"

"I'm afraid not. I've been going through Gail's notes. There's something we're missing, but my brain is refusing to cooperate. I was hoping you'd come up with it."

"Not yet," Allison confessed. "I guess I'll have to go down to the basement to do my thinking."

"Why the basement? I would think after your recent ordeal you'd never want to see another basement or cellar."

"My basement is actually a rec room and that's where my swivel chair is. It's almost like the one in your office. I use it to watch the kids play ping-pong, but maybe it'll stimulate my crime-solving juices."

But it wasn't the swivel chair which got the pot boiling— it was the bathtub. Later that night Allison was soaking in her "Golden Vanilla" bubble bath, making swirling designs with her right big toe and imagining she was floating in the waters off Bali. Her eyes were half closed and her brain was in neutral. Without warning, the lost list of clues began dancing before her face.

Her mind clawed at the scribbled notes she'd made in the library at the Blue Goose: each suspect's name, comments or questions after each one, some general questions. Many of the questions had been answered during the course of the investigation; some had not.

Allison blocked everything except the unanswered questions out of her consciousness: her bruised and painful shoulder, her stinging scratches, the burning sensation in her throat, the haunting smell of smoke. She immersed her body in the bubbles, her mind in the cosmos.

Several minutes later, she sat straight up, splashing water over the side of the tub. "Of course, that's it! How could I have been such a dunce?" Her mind grasped at conversations she'd had with various suspects. She recalled their statements, and the notes that Gail had taken. It all made sense now. Allison scrambled out of the tub, grabbed a towel on the way to the phone, and dialed Fred's number.

Without even a preliminary, "Hello," she shouted into the phone, "You need to check on two things for me."

"And who would this be?" Fred's voice feigned frostiness. "The Queen of England?"

Allison snickered. "Oh, I'm sorry, Your Honor. For a moment I forgot I was just a junior partner in this detective business. Let me rephrase my request. If you will please check on two items for me, I will then reveal the murderer to you. Does that sound better?"

"Much better. I'm at your service, Ma'am." After listening to Allison's request and explanation, Fred was all business. "I'll get back to you tomorrow."

All that night and the next morning Allison kept going over the case, mumbling to herself, "I know I'm right. But what if I'm wrong? But I can't be wrong. What if Fred doesn't find what I think he'll find, then even if I'm right, we won't be able to prove it?"

It was late afternoon when Fred called back. By that time, Allison had sworn to herself, her ancestors, and any grandchildren she might someday have, that never again would she play detective. "My nerves can't take this," she explained to the hall mirror. Her face was the color of milk of magnesia, her eyes were blood streaked, and her lips raw from constant clenching.

"This is your partner in crime reporting in, Inspector Aldridge," Fred said as she answered the phone.

Allison was in no mood for games. "Come off it, Fred. Was I right or not?"

Fred took a deep breath. Allison couldn't tell if he was preparing to congratulate her or let her down easily. The answer finally came. "Right as rain."

It was Allison's turn to inhale the sweet breath of victory and she decided she'd been a little hasty in turning her back on detective work. This was beginning to be fun again. "So now comes the arrest?"

"It's a little more complicated than that," Fred said. "We have a good circumstantial case, but I'm not sure it's enough to hold up in court."

Allison had a hard time getting past Fred's use of "we" and the warm feeling it brought her, but then she connected with the rest of the sentence. "What else do we need?"

"A confession would be nice," Fred said, "but there's little chance of that. People who premeditate murder seldom get guilt-ridden and feel the need to cleanse their souls."

Allison realized she was clutching the phone and

her right hand was starting to cramp. She switched hands. "So now what?"

"I'm not sure. I wish I could come up with some pretense for needing them all together again. That way we could question everyone without tipping our hand to the real suspect."

"You mean like Poirot's grand denouement scenes?"

"Something like that. I know such a scene sounds like a worn-out cliche, but in this case it might just work. The murderer might make another slip." Allison wished she could see Fred at the other end of the line. She liked the way his forehead wrinkled when he was deep in thought. His voice brought her back to attention. "Gail will accuse me of grand-standing, but she's said worse about me before. Maybe I could hatch something up with the family lawyer."

"Now that's an idea," Allison jumped in. "He could say he needed them there to survey the fire damage and determine what they want to do about repairs, contents of the house and so forth. They'll have to make some decisions soon anyway." Allison was excited about seeing all the suspects again and watching Fred work up to the climax of the case.

Then the dismal thought came to her that he wouldn't need her. He had all the information now. She asked hesitantly, "Could I come too?"

Fred laughed. "You know I couldn't keep you away if I barred the doors." His voice softened. "Besides, I miss you."

Allison lowered the phone and did a little twist step. "Yes-s-s," she whispered and couldn't disguise the lilt in her voice when she said, "Just tell me when."

NINETEEN

A FEW DAYS LATER the cousins gathered again in the library. Mr. McCabe, Bess's attorney and executor of her will, had gone along with Fred's plans. Actually, the lawyer had said it would be helpful to him if the heirs could come to an amicable agreement regarding the future of the estate and what repairs should be made. They were to meet at two o'clock. Fred, Gail, and Allison would arrive later and wait until an appropriate time to make their unannounced entrances.

When they drove up, Fred noted that the front part of the lodge appeared to be intact. Plywood panels were nailed up over the back and tarps were stretched across the roof. He wondered what the future had in store for the decrepit lodge. But right now his mind had to stay on the task at hand. He had a murderer to trap.

All went according to plan. After the cousins had their say, and as Mr. McCabe was winding up his legal spiel, Fred slammed the back door, winked at Allison, and barged into the room with Gail right behind him. Two uniformed officers waited in the hallway. Allison slipped quietly into a corner seat.

Without apology, Fred faced the family. There was Charles, handsome as ever, but looking pale and worn. His white tee shirt advertised an Earth Week that had occurred over a year ago. And either he had neglected to shave for several days, or he was trying to grow a beard. At any rate, he looked like he would rather have been on a desert island than in a stuffy library.

Catherine's face, on the other hand, was settled in peaceful repose. She wore a loose striped skirt with patch pockets where her hands rested comfortably.

Teddy sat next to the coffee table where Lillian had thoughtfully left a plate of cookies and a pitcher of tea. He wore casual slacks, a paisley shirt, and a pained expression. Fred noticed Imogene's color-coordinated outfit: a yellow short sleeve blouse, a black and white vest, black slacks, white Nikes with yellow laces, and yellow socks. Her carbon black hair was pulled back with a perky yellow ribbon. He smiled at her. Imogene frowned back, leaned over and handed Teddy another cookie.

Derita's hair seemed a shade lighter than Fred remembered it and a bit more windblown. She looked utterly bored.

"I hope no one is in a hurry to leave," the detective started, "because I have a few more questions to ask. Easier here than having to look each one of you up separately. However, I'm not detaining anyone. If you wish to leave, you may. In which case, I can contact you later."

No one got up to leave. No one argued. The

innocent ones had no reason to object and the guilty one was probably either afraid to make waves or was very cocky.

Gail sat at the desk, but this time instead of a notebook, she flipped on a tape recorder. Fred explained, "In the interest of accuracy, we'll record our session." Again no one objected. Fred studied the five people in front of him. A sadness came over him: a sadness that there were such greedy people in the world they would kill to get what they wanted, a sadness that the revelation of the murderer would bring heartache to the innocent ones, a sadness that time could never be reversed and there was nothing to do but to go forward.

So he went forward. "Derita, tell me again your version of events the night of the murder. There are a couple of points I'm not clear about."

If Derita was upset or intimidated by the request, she didn't show it. She gave a resigned nod of her head. "Fine. Where do you want me to start?"

"Let's start when you said you gave your aunt her bedtime medications."

Derita scowled. "I didn't say I gave her medicines. I said I got her some fresh water and that she took her own medicines later."

"She poured the pills from the bottles herself?"

"She must have. I didn't touch them." Fred thought Derita was beginning to sound flustered.

"What about her inhaler and nasal spray?"

"What about them?" Derita's voice was now defiant.

"Did she use either of them while you were in the room?"

"No. She may have used them after I left. They were within her reach on the bedside table."

"Did you see them when you went in to close the window?" Fred left no pauses between one answer and the next question.

Derita, in turn, answered each question quickly and without hesitation. "It was dark. I couldn't see anything except the faint light out the window and the outline of her body in the bed."

"Body?" Fred repeated. "Why did you say body? Was she already dead?"

Derita shook her head at the detective and gave him a tired smile. "I think you're trying to trick me, Sir. Let me rephrase that. All I could see was her sleeping body in bed. Now don't you think you've been on my case long enough? What about the others?"

The others had all been staring at Derita as if she was putting on a one-man show at a dinner theater. "I'll get to them in a moment," Fred said. "Just two more questions. Are you sure you heard your aunt speak to you at nine-thirty?"

"Yes."

"And what were her exact words?"

"She said, 'I'm okay. Leave me alone.'"

Charles stirred. Fred looked at him. "Did you have something to add?"

Charles started to shake his head and then apparently changed his mind. His voice was low and apologetic. "But Aunt Bess never used the word 'okay.' She insisted it was slang."

"That's right," Teddy blurted out. "She was always correcting me for saying it."

Derita rolled her eyes in disgust. "So maybe those weren't her exact words. But she said something like that. Her voice was low. It doesn't matter what she said. The fact that she said anything proves she was alive at that time."

Fred made no comment to this. "My last question to you, Derita, is why didn't you hear your aunt thrashing about in bed during the night and knocking over her medicine bottles? Serena told us she found all her bottles on the floor. It's a hardwood floor. I would think the falling bottles would have made considerable noise."

"One would think so. But the fact is, I didn't hear anything after I went to bed."

"That fact is," Fred paused, turned his back on Derita and faced the others, "that Derita didn't hear the bottles fall because the event had occurred earlier, probably when she was downstairs. Bess Lattimer was already dead at nine-thirty. She was dead when Derita claimed to hear her speak. She was dead when Derita entered the room to close the window."

"But how?" The words seemed to come from all the cousins at the same time.

"We have Allison to thank for figuring that out. She had the right clues; it just took her a while to put them together in the right order."

Fred then turned to Teddy and Imogene. "Imogene, I understand you're a good actress."

Imogene caught a quick breath, glanced at Teddy, and then returned Fred's steady gaze. "Yes. I'm a very good actress. So?"

"You're especially talented in changing your voice. You can sound like a child. You can sound like an old woman. Maybe you were in Bess's room when Derita opened the bathroom door after her shower. Perhaps it was your voice Derita heard instead of her aunt's."

"That's ridiculous. Why would I be in the room?" Imogene held her head high, flipped her pony tail and pasted on a thin mysterious smile. Fred sensed that the accused was no longer just Imogene Faircloth, but had shifted into her actress mode. Imogene was on stage and enjoying it immensely.

Fred took a deep breath and went on. "Before we go any further, Imogene, Gail is going to inform you of your rights and, then if you wish, we can finish this at the station with your lawyer present."

Teddy's head jerked up, his mouth flew open, he gasped for breath. Imogene patted his hand and her smile widened as she listened to Gail's legal litany. At the end, Imogene gave her attention back to Fred, "So now I know my rights, and I'm not afraid to answer any of your questions. Go ahead. Why do you think I was in Bess's room?"

"You were in the room to switch back the nasal spray bottles. You had to retrieve the one with the poison in it which you had planted earlier, and replace it with another. You knew Bess used the spray at night to help her breathe easier. You knew one sniff of the cyanide in the bottle would likely kill her."

"But you forget I was in my own room watching TV. Teddy can vouch for that." Imogene turned to her husband. "Remember, honey, you came in at the end of the Errol Flynn movie." Teddy nodded, but didn't say anything. His eyes turned from his wife to Fred to the floor.

"But you told us yourself that Teddy went down to the kitchen to get something to eat," Fred said. "In fact, you're the one who reminded your husband about the leftover banana pudding. When Teddy went downstairs, you sneaked into Bess's room, saw that she was dead, picked up the poison bottle, and replaced it with another. You were probably fearful the poisoned one might still be dangerous so you tossed it out the window. We found the screen pushed open at the bottom. It would have been simple for you to retrieve the bottle from the yard the next morning and then quickly hide it in the garage. You didn't take time to pick up the other medicine bottles because you had to get back to your room before Teddy returned. However, you did take time to close the window when you heard Derita say she would come in later to close it. You may have thought she would notice the screen."

Teddy rose, fists clenched, breathing heavily. "Lies! That's all lies!"

Fred seemed to take no notice of Teddy's threatening stance. He shook his head sadly. "No, it's all true. You see, we found the murder weapon. There was still cyanide in the spray bottle. And we also found the pipe used to hit both Becky and Allison."

Fred's stare returned to Imogene's face. The actress was still in control. She pulled Teddy back to his seat and patted his hand as if soothing a fretful child. "Don't worry, honey. He can't prove a thing."

Fred looked around the room at the other cousins. Charles was gripping the arms of his chair so hard the veins of his hands stood out like gnarled ropes and under his stubble of whiskers, his chin trembled. Derita was shaking her head in apparent disbelief while Catherine kept her eyes on Teddy.

"Maybe I forgot to mention," Fred went on, "that we also found fingerprints."

The actress mask evaporated. "That's impossible!" Imogene screamed. "You made that up. There were no fingerprints on the bottle."

The very room seemed to quiver with the collective gasps of its occupants.

Teddy pushed Imogene's hand away. "How would you know that?" he asked his wife.

Charles nodded his head. "Only the murderer would know that the bottle had been wiped clean."

"Not necessarily," Derita chimed in, her voice implying that it was time to listen to some common sense. "Any murderer worth his salt would wipe his fingerprints off the weapon. Imogene knows that as well as the rest of us." Imogene and Teddy both looked at Derita with thankful eyes.

Catherine, who up until now hadn't said a word

during the inquisition, broke her silence. "Maybe it can't be proved, Imogene, but I know you did it. I know in my gut you killed Aunt Bess. I knew it couldn't have been one of my cousins. You may even have rationalized that you were doing it for Teddy, to save his business. But you were doing it for yourself. If Teddy had lost his business, his money, then he wouldn't be able to back the stage production he'd promised you. Lillian was right when she said you only cared about your acting and your jewelry."

Catherine turned sad eyes to her younger cousin. "I'm sorry, Teddy, but the truth must come out. I could almost forgive her for Aunt Bess, but not for what she did to Becky and Allison."

The effort had been too much for Catherine. The skirt where she had hidden her hands began flailing like a kite in a wind storm. Allison went over and held her friend tightly until the trembling lessened.

Fred again took over the stage before anyone else could speak. "As I was saying, Imogene, we found fingerprints." He could tell Imogene was trying to get back into her actress mode, but didn't quite make it before Fred fired the next shot. "They weren't on the spray bottle. They were on the container of cyanide where you got the poison."

Imogene sat back in her chair, her eyes wary and fearful. She reached again for Teddy's hand and he allowed her to cling to him as Fred continued, "You told Allison about the jewelry you designed and you boasted that you were permitted to wander around the factory, that you could even steal some of the pure gold if you wanted to. However, it wasn't their gold you stole, but the cyanide they use in the jewelry-making process. It's kept in closed containers clearly marked as poison. At night it's securely locked. During the day it's available for use. You must have realized how easy it would be to sneak some out."

ALLISON RETURNED TO her corner chair where she could monitor all the action. She looked at Fred with pride. He was so professional, so sure of himself. Allison wished she felt as confident as Fred looked. Could he really prove that Imogene was the killer?

Allison noticed tears beginning to trickle down Teddy's cheeks. He took the hand which Imogene grasped and swiped the side of his face. Imogene seemed not to notice. She scooted toward the edge of her chair and straightened her shoulders.

Fred didn't pause. "You had decided to kill your husband's aunt after your visit here in April. You knew she wasn't going to agree to his development plan. You had ample opportunity to examine her medicines and decided the nasal spray would work well. Your next step was to obtain the needed poison. It wasn't hard. You took some sketches of jewelry to the plant, told them you needed a special piece for a special occasion and then, as you had in the past, you wandered around the plant greeting the workers. You had, no doubt, a suitable container on your person or in your purse in which to place a small amount of cyanide. Several prints were found on the lid of the container. All the prints, except one, matched those of the personnel authorized to use the substance. The one other print was yours, Imogene."

"We've got her," Allison muttered to herself. "She can't get out of it now."

Allison was wrong. Imogene rallied like the mythical phoenix. "I may have touched the lid as I wandered around the plant," she said, her head again held high, "but there's no proof I took anything out of the container."

Allison was aghast as Fred dropped his head as if conceding defeat. Imogene's smile widened. She's going to enjoy this stage victory to the very end, Allison thought. What can Fred say to that? But Fred didn't have to say anything, Imogene did it for him. "And you can't prove I used the cyanide to make the poison gas." Allison caught Fred's grin under his bowed head. She knew this was the kind of slip-up he'd been waiting for. No one in the family had been told about the cyanide powder being converted to a gas. They knew about the nasal spray bottle because Becky had identified it, but not about the gas. The innocent ones probably assumed, as the police did at first, that the cyanide itself had entered the nasal tract and had been absorbed into the tissues.

Fred lifted his head, but didn't immediately point out Imogene's slip. "You were in a production a few years ago entitled *Death Row*. It was about a killer awaiting death in the gas chamber. Unfortunately, the playwright described the exact procedure for making

Prussic Acid or Hydrocyanic Acid, the kind of gas used in executions. The play, incidentally, got good reviews." Fred smiled at Imogene and this time she smiled back.

"Yes, it did," Imogene said. "My performance was compared to Julia Roberts in some of her more demanding roles."

"I know," Fred went on, "the reviews were faxed to me just before I left the office—along with pages from the script which included the poison gas recipe, thanks to your most cooperative director. I also talked to him and he mentioned the odd coincidence of you asking him last spring for a copy of that script. You said you had mislaid yours and wanted it for your scrapbook."

Imogene blanched, her complexion now matched the white part of her vest. "That still doesn't prove…" she started.

Fred held up his hand. He was through playing games. "You're a very good actress, Imogene, but you slipped up on one of your lines. There's no way you could have known the cyanide was converted to a poison gas unless you had done it yourself."

Mr. McCabe had stayed around and now re-entered the library. He addressed Teddy. "Would you like me to recommend a criminal attorney?"

Teddy kept his eyes on the floor, nodded, and whispered in a hoarse voice, "Yes, please."

TWENTY

TWO OFFICERS entered the library. Fred had instructed them to stay out of sight until time for the arrest. Catherine got up and hugged Teddy as he staggered after his wife. Then the other cousins fled the house. Allison joined them on the front porch as Fred and Gail stayed behind to go over some details.

"Poor Teddy," Derita was saying. "He really loves her, you know." She stared out at the tranquil lake, a sadness on her face Allison had never seen before. "I wonder what it would be like to be loved unconditionally—no matter what."

"It's rare. Extremely rare." Charles grimaced and rubbed the back of his neck.

Allison looked around. We've all been hurt by love, she thought, or the lack of it. I guess that's the gamble you take in this world. You pay your money and take a chance. Some lucky people holler, "BINGO!" while others dump their cards in disgust. A few, like Derita, keep trying. Others give up and quit. Allison wasn't sure which category she was in yet.

FRED CAME OUT and plopped in the nearest porch chair. He had no sense of triumph, no elation that the case had been solved, not even an inner pleasure that justice had prevailed. He simply felt exhausted. He closed his eyes and hoped for a moment's peace. It was not to be.

Charles sat on the porch steps, his back against the railing, the front of his tee shirt damp where he had used it to wipe his tears. Charles was of that rare breed of men who hadn't forgotten how to cry. "But I don't understand how she could have hurt my little Becky," he said.

"That's the problem with murder," Fred sighed. "The evil keeps spreading like an oil spill. It keeps on spoiling, contaminating, killing whatever is in its path." Fred shook himself back to the present situation. "I'm sorry, Charles. I know you want answers, not philosophy. The only answer seems to be self-preservation. I assume Imogene hadn't yet wiped her fingerprints off the bottle when Becky found it, so she had to get it away. She didn't see Becky as a little girl or as your daughter. Becky was only an obstacle to her, an obstacle which had to be removed."

"But why Allison?" Catherine asked. "Allison was no threat to her."

"Oh, but she was," Fred said. "Allison had written out a list of the suspects and comments about each one. One of the questions pointed directly to Imogene, although neither Allison nor I realized it at the time. Imogene, however, knew that sooner or later the truth would dawn on Allison. So Imogene tried to eliminate her. Eventually the truth did dawn and that's how Allison solved the case." He looked in Allison's direction. "It's your story. Want to finish it?"

Allison shook her head. "Go ahead. You're doing fine."

Fred continued. "Allison had written the question next to Derita's name, but then realized it was in the wrong place. She had written, 'did she really hear Bess's voice about nine-thirty?' A simple enough question. Allison wondered if Derita was telling the truth, but Imogene thought Allison was suspicious that the voice belonged to someone other than Bess. And since Derita's name appeared right after hers, Imogene was afraid it wouldn't be long before Allison figured out whose voice it was. Most likely, Imogene recalled telling Allison about her range of acting roles."

Fred went on, "We may never know exactly what happened that night of the first attack on Allison, but we can flesh out what little information we do have. Allison throws the list of clues toward the trash can, then walks down to the lake and sits on the pier. Remember, she's here alone. Teddy and Imogene drive up intending to spend the night. Teddy makes a beeline for the kitchen. Imogene waits in the library for him to finish eating. She sees the paper on the floor, picks it up, reads it, knows she's in trouble. Perhaps she looks around for Allison, probably goes out to the porch and sees Allison on the pier. It's dark. Imogene is still dressed in black. It isn't likely she'll be seen. She retrieves the weapon she'd used on

Becky from wherever she'd hidden it, creeps down the hill, and does the dirty deed. She buries the pipe in the sand under the pier and makes her way back to the house. Teddy is finished eating and she tells him she doesn't want to spend the night here, and so they go back to a motel.

"Then another chance presents itself for Imogene to get rid of the potential threat. She learns Allison is returning here to get the cat. She decides to try one more time. She, no doubt, heard Teddy on the phone telling Catherine where Allison could find the cat carrier. As soon as Teddy leaves that morning, she takes off to come here. She probably parks the car somewhere in the woods where it won't be seen. She waits for Allison, locks her in the cellar and starts the fire, thinking Allison will either die in the flames or from the smoke. Imogene then hurries back to Charlotte and buys something in an old, established dress shop; she knows their register tapes don't record the time of the sale. Then she sits back, relaxes and thinks her troubles are over."

Fred pauses to let his audience appreciate his deductions. "We may not be able to prove all that, however," he adds. "Unfortunately, the dress shop clerk thinks she remembers Imogene being in that day, but doesn't remember the time. But," he smiled, "we still have an ace in the hole. I have men checking gas stations between here and Charlotte. She must have gotten gas somewhere along the way coming or going. When we find out where, then we can prove she wasn't shopping all day as she alleges."

"But the jewelry, the script?" Derita asked. "How

did you find out about them? More of Allison's superb detective work?"

"Exactly. But it was actually Imogene's need to boast of her accomplishments that did her in. She'd told Allison about the death-row play and then went on to tell her about her jewelry designs. Allison gave me the leads and I followed up."

Charles stood up. "Well, at least it's over."

"Except for Teddy," Catherine said. "It'll never be over for him."

FRED MOTIONED ALLISON to follow him down to the lakeside. They strolled in silence, past the swing, out onto the pier. The water was glassy smooth; the water lilies leaves lazed out like green pancakes, their blossoms resembling blobs of butter ready to melt in the afternoon heat. Allison looked over toward Jake's place and spied a papa swan swimming in protective circles around his mate and their fledgling cygnets. Overhead, a gray hawk soared and swooped, intent on filching an evening snack. "It's an enchanting lake," Allison said. "I'll remember it fondly in spite of all that happened here."

"I hope you'll remember something else fondly besides the lake." Fred dug in his shirt pocket and hauled out a scrap of paper. "Like this, for instance." He handed the paper to Allison.

"What's this?"

"A haiku. I thought I'd try my hand at writing one." Fred shrugged and held out his hands. "It's not much of a thank-you gift, but it's all I could come up with."

Allison opened the slip of paper, swiped back a tear. "That is so sweet of you."

"It's probably not any good. But it's about nature and it's seventeen syllables and well—just go ahead and read it."

Allison read softly.

Hot summer roadways
Jack rabbits dodge tall, dry weeds
And Budweiser cans.

She gave Fred a huge smile. "It's good. It's very good." Without realizing even what she was going to do, Allison reached up and soundly kissed him on the cheek. "It's one of the best gifts I've ever received." At a later time, she thought, and she was sure there would be a later time, she would suggest he substitute *Queen Anne's Lace* for *tall, dry weeds,* but for now it was perfect. It was perfect because he cared enough to try to share her love of poetry. But what could she give him?

"I didn't actually get a thank-you gift for you for letting me play detective," Allison said as she tunneled into her handbag and came out with a brown wrapper, "but would you like to split a Snickers?"